AMAZON/PRINT VERSION ONLY

EBOOK/PRINT COVER: CAROL MARQUES DESIGN
EDITING, PROOFING, BACKGROUNDS, & FORMATTING: DIRTY SEXY WORDS/ STORM SHIELD EDITING/LITTLE TAILFEATHER PUBLISHING
CASSANDRA /LTF LOGOS: PRETTY IN INK CREATIONS/ARTLOGO
GOOSEBUSTERS ALPHA TEAM: KAT SILVER, BECKY ROSS, ERICA TARYN
DUCKHUNTERS PROOFERS: JACKIE H
SENSITIVITY READERS: BRIT MASON, GAIL JERICHO
LEGAL SERVICES: JOSHUA FARLEY, ESQ.
REPRESENTATION: LAURA PINK AT SBR MEDIA
IMAGES/FONTS: CREATIVE FABRICA, DEPOSITPHOTOS, SHUTTERSTOCK, & PHOTOSHOP

NO GENAI WAS USED WITHIN THIS BOOK. ALL ERRORS AND GREATNESS ARE BY AN ADHD MUPPET.

Content Information

This is a *paranormal whychoose romance with poly elements*—our FMC, Delores, will not have to choose between love interests.

There are many situations included that are intended for mature audiences (18+).

In this book, there may be instances/references (be they small or lengthy) that could trigger some individuals such as:

- loss of virginity between two 18 year olds that some consider dubious consent (I do not see it as such, but based on reader feedback I am listing it.)
- biting
- traumatic childhood
- MF, MM, and more pairings in futures books
- super heinous puns (seriously, lots)
- underage drinking
- drug use
- unhealthy coping mechanisms
- neurospicy MMC
- death

- body modifications
- slightly unhinged MMC
- bullying (in person and on social media)
- blood
- emotional abuse from parents and friends
- alcohol abuse
- domestic violence
- implied child abuse
- body dysmorphia
- adult language
- emotional manipulation
- adorable nicknames
- physical intimidation
- voyeurism
- masturbation
- professors/student (above 18+)
- age gap (from 17 yrs to almost 2000 yrs)
- family dysfunction
- betrayal (non-poly group)
- absolute disrespect for shitty parents
- pop culture references (so many)
- brief mentions of non-body positive dieting culture
- discussion of other species as lower
- official corruption
- name calling
- occasional misogyny
- inappropriate use of a library
- exhibitionism
- adult bullying
- elitism
- bribery
- corpses
- fat shaming (not by MCs)
- drama
- physical threats to FMC and others
- species-ism

- non-consensual drugging
- discussion of arranged marriages

No sexual practices in this book should be taken as safe or appropriate for real life application.

Content information is important and I don't ever want to harm a reader with inaccurate information.

Stalk Cassandra Featherstone in the Dark Corners of the Web

Join my Facebook group and follow me everywhere!

Want More?

Sign up for my bi-weekly manifesto for a free series sampler:

Author Ramblings

Readers,

If you've read my solo books, you know I take great pride in my work. You also know that 2021 was a *rough* year for me, despite several successful releases in multiple series. There are many reasons for that, both personally and professionally, but I have finally gotten my life back.

That's why this re-release is so vitally important to me.

When authors write books, we make a lot of concessions to meet expectations from editors, readers, reviewers, the market, and our genre. If you toss in other variables, it becomes even trickier to get your vision to the page in an iteration you're completely happy with. You make concessions to meet expectations from everyone, even if it means compromising on points when you disagree with them.

The Apex series is an example of such a situation. There are a plethora of reasons the series is being revamped under my brand alone and not all of them are for public consumption. However, now that it is, I can adjust the things I've been dreaming up and

I'm beyond ecstatic to bring you the new Apex Society universe.

I re-wrote and edited *Come Out & Prey* to reflect the adjustments to the series that I'm titling '*Apex Academy Capers.*' These books are part of the first series that will take place in the larger *Apex Society Adventures* universe. If you read the previously released editions, you will find some major changes within the pages and some things will be familiar. As stated previously, I cannot go into detail about the reasoning for this, but I ask you to have an open mind while you read.

Change is necessary in order for us to grow.

I am very proud of the achievements I've earned since I started publishing in 2020, and despite the bump in the road this represents, I believe I am continually improving. None of us are perfect and we all make mistakes—even with the best intentions. It doesn't mean we have to give up; rather, we buckle our armor and push once more into the breach.

That's what I've done with this set of my darlings and I hope you love the result as much as I do.

For the past three years, I have been learning more about craft, my business, and networking in order to grow my brand so I can go full time. One of the hardest realizations during this time was that you cannot take anything for granted and you always have to protect both yourself and your business—even when it seems unnecessary. You cannot let others dictate the trajectory of your career, no matter how much you trust or like them personally. Everything in this industry can turn on a dime, even relationships.

I am looking forward to my third year of publishing, even with this in mind. The series I have running and the individuals I'm currently working with are outstanding from co-writer to cover artists to consultants and even my amazeballs lawyer. (Don't hold that or the fact that he played trumpet in high school against him, guys; he's a great dude.) My readers, betas, alphas, arc teams and fans are the best— a fact I'm eternally grateful for because I know

I'm a *bit much* occasionally.

I'll leave you with a few parting words to consider:

Guard your peace.

Stand your ground.

Validate yourself.

Protect your brand.

Don't be a dick.

… and whatever you do, don't forget the sunscreen.

Blood and guts,

Cassandra Featherstone
QUEEN OF SMART, SASSY SPICE

READER'S NOTE

A FEW THINGS YOU SHOULD KNOW...

Come Out & Prey should be read *before* the first book, *Let Us Prey.* It is not a 'throwaway' prequel; it sets up the world in which our characters live for the first book.

This is a multi-book series, so *I will not reveal everything in the first book.* Some plot lines will continue through series in a larger arc and not get resolved in the first or even the next book. I promise it will all get tied up and have a HEA; don't worry!

Come Out & Prey is a why choose/poly romance, which means our FMC will not have to choose. I would consider it a medium burn, slow build family group. It will get spicier in the following books. If you're looking for porn with little to no plot, no judgment, but this isn't the series for you. It's also not closed door or FTB, so I believe the spice will be worth the wait. I realize spice scales are subjective and everyone has different opinions on it, so forgive me if mine and yours aren't totally aligned.

There are some characters and creatures that speak in other languages. I made the *translations clickable end-of-chapter notes* to help.

Just an FYI:

There are a *lot of puns*—they are intentionally bad at times and writing them made me giggle. If you don't like silly, world-specific humor like that, it may annoy you.

There are some words that are slang, jargon, or foreign that may seem to be spelled wrong—*please email the author or find her on social media rather than report to Amazon* if you find a typo. This has been proofed and edited *several* times since release; if you believe you found errors, you may not be correct. It could be a stylistic choice or a dialect choice. Please do not assume the two ARC teams, betas, alphas, and several proofers missed everything you believe is incorrect.

Please do not email critical feedback that is not a simple typo or formatting issue—this book is written and released. It will not be changed after publication to suit personal editing opinions or requests.

If you see this book *anywhere besides Kindle Unlimited in ebook format,* please reach out to me via social media or email. Pirating kills my ability to write full time and I am so grateful for your help.

Contact my team for typos or to report piracy: teamcassandrafeatherstone@cassandrafeatherstone.com

COME OUT & PREY PLAYLIST

CHAPTER TITLE SONGS

Come Out & Prey Chapter Playlist

BONUS PLAYLIST

Delores' In Another Life Playlist

"Bullying is a cowardly act. It's easy to bully someone when they aren't looking or when they can't fight back."

-Anonymous

Just A Girl

Delores

Sighing, I look around my bedroom at the posters and decorations covering my walls. My obsession with pop music, musical theater, and high school rom-coms sickens my parents. They would prefer me to be into heavy metal and horror movies, like the other kids my age.

Being the only child in a family as prominent as mine is difficult when you don't fit the mold. My parents—like their parents and all my friends' parents—are apex predators. Preds rule our world, and the division between us and prey is so severe that we regulate them to a completely different echelon of society. Prey shifters are weak and beneath our lofty abilities. The ruling class of elite predator families stretches back generations, and they've evolved into a bunch of assholes who only care about succession and greed.

My animal has not manifested yet, but it will soon enough. Luckily for me, none of my friends have manifested their inner animals, either. I'm part of the in-crowd at school, and my boyfriend, Todd, is the most popular guy in my class. While he and I aren't officially engaged yet, we've talked about it enough that I know it's only a matter of time before he puts a ring on my finger. I should be on top of the world, but I can't help but feel like my life just doesn't fit me the way it's supposed to.

Every teenager wishes their life was different, but I dream of becoming an entirely different person. Not inside, mind, because I'm pretty comfortable with who I am. I don't want to be part of this legacy, this society, or even this family. They are all focused on competing to be the richest, the deadliest, or the most powerful, and I want no part of it.

I walk over to my closet and pull out the outfit that I had chosen for my tour of Apex Academy. My mother hired her personal designers to create a custom school uniform for today and expects me to present the 'appropriate' image of the sole heir to a Council seat.

I hate having to pretend to be like them because I'm nothing like them.

Regardless, I pull on the short, pink pleated skirt, three quarter length sleeve blouse, knee socks, and Mary Janes that comprise the uniform for my exclusive private high school. Since I'm using a 'college visit' day to tour the Academy, I'm expected to represent Shifter Secondary as well.

Shifter Secondary is the most exclusive high school for unmanifested shifter teens on the East Coast. Unfortunately for me, it was not my parents' first choice for my education. They hoped I'd follow in their footsteps by choosing to force my animal to emerge early. If I had done that, I could have attended *Apex Academy Lower School*.

I didn't have the stomach to use my body in that manner at fourteen.

Their heirs followed my lead, which made my mother and father furious and their hoity-toity council colleagues angry. My closest friends, the Heathers, also refused to force their animals to emerge, as did Todd and his friends. That was the first time the adults in our circle decided I was a bad influence. After that, I had to toe the line at every turn, ensuring that I followed all the strict rules and regulations that govern the heirs to council seats.

Everywhere I went, I had to dress in a manner befitting the next Drew to sit at the table. They forced me to take dance lessons, piano lessons, diction lessons, and other more humiliating tutorials to prepare for the day that I became a true predator. In our society, teenagers have no say in how we prepare for our animals to emerge.

Your parents make all the decisions, choose your friends, choose your mates, and decide every detail of your life down to what you eat every single day. At least, that's how it is in my family, because my mother is from the old world.

She came over from Slovenia when she was incredibly young and met my father on the society fundraiser circuit. Her idea of preparing her daughter for the future involves lessons in makeup, clothing, jewelry, and on how to keep your mate satisfied. Lucille is completely unconcerned about whether I end up happy, only that I attend to my council seat and my husband's *needs*.

Once I get dressed, I grab my vintage Vuitton bag and peek at the mirror for a last check before I head downstairs. I tuck my perfectly highlighted blonde tresses behind my ears, and the smokey eye and winged liner are on point with this year's fashion trends. I apply a quick swipe of cherry red lip gloss and open my mouth, inspecting my teeth to make sure they are pearly white. Even though once I develop threatening incisors or sharp fangs, something will inevitably cover them in blood, my parents want my smile to look like a toothpaste commercial.

It's all such utter bullshit.

I take a deep breath and turn on my heel, heading for the door. I can already hear my parents yelling in a Scotch and vodka induced rage in the drawing room. It's only eleven thirty in the morning, for Hera's sake.

Lucille and Bruno don't fuck around with cocktail hour. They are nicely sauced by ten a.m. every day, without exception. I can't remember a time when my parents didn't get drunk off their asses at an event or party, much less in our 'home'. They liquor up and fight until they part for the day, and then start again once they arrive home from their daily commitments.

I brace for the barrage of criticism my mother will subject me to when I cross the threshold. Closing my eyes, I whisper words of encouragement to myself via lyrics to some of my favorite songs, desperately trying to hype myself up before she can tear me down.

"Delores! I hear you breathing at the top of the stairs, darling. Come down this instant and let your father and I inspect your presentation."

My mother's purr *sounds* friendly, but believe me, it's not. I roll my eyes as I make my way down the stairs, knowing my mother won't hesitate to send one of the staff if I don't acquiesce to her command. Most of their staff would gleefully jizz themselves with being chosen to drag me downstairs for inspection.

At this time of day, the only servant in the drawing room will be Matilda—my ex-nanny turned personal assistant—and that request would test her loyalties. As the only person in my household who has my back, I don't want to put her in that position, so I answer. "Yes, Lucille. I'm on my way."

I'm not allowed to refer to her as 'mother' because it makes her feel old. 'Lucille' is always what I've called the woman who supposedly gave birth to me. I'd be tempted to disbelieve we shared any DNA at all if it weren't for our similar bone structure. She's about as nurturing as a rattlesnake, and if it weren't for Matilda, I might have died as a child. If the kitchen staff whispers are accurate, I have to accept that my mother neglected to feed me much of the time.

"You coddle her far too much, Lucille," my father growls. "As the heir to our family seat, Delores will come without being instructed to do so. We will not tolerate her insolence after her animal emerges. She will behave as I command or suffer the consequences."

The last of Bruno's rant echoes off the marble walls of the foyer as I step onto the hideously expensive, endangered teak floor. Schooling my features into the mask of indifference I wear whenever I have to deal with them, I enter their den of drunken fights with my spine steeled for an emotional assault.

"I apologize for my tardiness, Father. I only wished to perfect the image I will present during my tour of Apex Academy. I realize it is imperative I impress the Headmistress and her staff."

The humanoid features of his face shift seamlessly, and the hungry crocodile inside of him gives me a toothy smirk. "You will impress them, daughter, or so help me… I'll send you to Bloodstone Isle."

My stomach drops like a stone as I barely suppress a shiver.

Bloodstone Isle is a reformatory school. It's surrounded by spells and enchantments to prevent students from escaping—a feat that has only happened once in its one thousand years of existence. The most feared cat group in the shifter world—the Khan ambush—runs the school, and they're rumored to consume errant students when the Council allows it.

It's the threat both rich and poor shifter parents used to keep their children in line. Wealthy parents like mine use it as a method of controlling any heirs that refuse to conform to the rigid structure of our society. Predators don't value the lives of those who are weak, and they label heirs who refuse to take their rightful place at the top of the food chain weak. Everyone knows Bloodstone is full of criminals, miscreants, and psychos, and even they don't seem to survive.

Bloodstone is a death sentence—pure and simple.

"Y-yes, Father. I understand," I croak out. As if the pressure of touring my new school isn't enough, now I worry the Dean will relay something to my parents that gets me shipped off to Death Island.

"Bruno, darling, if you scare her, she'll frown. That causes wrinkles. Delores, chin up and smile for us."

Swallowing the lump in my throat, I flash my mother my brightest smile. Her blood-red lips curve, and her leopard fangs burst free as she all but purrs. "I will not have you sullying the family name, Delores. It's bad enough that your education gave you ideas about your value beyond breeding stock. You will take the seat on the Council when it is time, but the husband we select will control the business—as nature intended. Do you hear me?"

My eyes narrow briefly, and for what is possibly the millionth time this week alone, I nod at my mother to appease her temper. "Yes, Lucille."

"Excellent!" The leopard fades as she claps her hands. "Matilda!"

The tiny woman steps up, her eyes wide behind her glasses. She's a pred, but being the smaller size of hawk shifters puts her in the servant class. I believe she genuinely lives in fear of one or both of my parents deciding to eat her. "Yes, madam?"

"Fetch Bruiser. He will accompany Delores to the academy for her tour. Tell him to take the Escalade—it won't do for her to arrive in a tiny car—it will draw attention to her extra weight. We must make an impression."

Matilda nods, and I feel the fear radiating from her, and I don't blame her. Bruiser is one of my parents' bodyguards and our frequent chauffeur. He's a Komodo dragon shifter and the house staff are terrified of him. It's hard not to be, given that he prefers to play with his food, then eat it after it's dead. The kitchen crew believes he 'handled' the gardener, who looked too long at my mother when I was ten. He disappeared without a trace.

Once Matilda scurries away, I watch my parents drink and bicker about their plans for the day. Bruno is going golfing with a congressman, and Lucille is going to the spa. We all know that both outings will include stops at the homes of their current pieces of ass for a quickie, but no one talks about it. The appearance of the loving couple has to be maintained, although neither of them has slept in the same room since I was a baby.

They don't give a damn about fidelity; I learned that at an early age. Children often discover things they shouldn't because adults discount their ability to understand the conversations happening around them.

I stopped keeping track of who they're boning long ago, because I'd need an assistant to keep the affairs straight.

While my parents' marriage is a sham, I remind myself that my boyfriend, Todd, isn't like them. Yes, his parents only own half the live entertainment industry, but my father allows me to see Todd. The other parents will force the Heathers to accept an arranged betrothal, and I'm grateful I'm lucky enough to have found the perfect match on my own as my high school sweetheart.

"Delores, Bruiser is ready to escort you to Apex. He's pulling the car around now," the hawk shifter says softly.

Snapping out of my reverie, I smile at the trembling woman. Bruiser must have scared the living hell out of her. For no other reason than it amused him, I'm sure. He's as much a brute as his name implies, and I don't look forward to riding alone to the academy with him.

Something about that shifter gives me the creeps…

Shake It Off

I spent the bulk of the drive to Apex Academy texting with Todd and the Heathers, while Bruiser muttered angrily to himself as he drove. He doesn't want to be here as much as me, so that makes us even.

Despite the common ground today, I don't trust him. Bruno gives him far too much responsibility for being what amounts to a beef-cake, and I suspect my parents tasked him with spying on me. Not that a six foot five, muscled brute in an Armani suit could be unobtrusive, but my father isn't stupid. He probably knows I'm on to Bruiser and figures there's more than one way to skin a cat.

My guess is Bruiser knows and enjoys all of them intimately.

I hop out of the car as soon as it stops in front of the massive Gothic style admissions building. I'm eager to ditch my shadow, find my friends, and commiserate about our ridiculous parents. If I'm honest, I complain more than the four Heathers, Todd, or his bros, but I have the worst of the bunch. At least the Heathers' parents aren't boffing every secretary, pool guy, and tennis pro in town. The boys couldn't care less what their mothers say, and their fathers are molding them like gilded trophies. I'm the only one considered a 'disappointment' to their family name, and the bad influence of the group.

It's unfair I'm taking all the heat when we all *agreed not to lose our virginity to force our beasts into early emergence.*

"DD!"

The high-pitched shout comes from the far side of the steps, and I squint, trying to determine which Heather it is. They're all coiffed and surgically enhanced to look like quadruplets, so I can't delineate them by appearance alone. I'm left with precious few options after that because the Heathers dress exactly alike, save one detail.

Every. Single. Day.

"I'm coming, Heather!" I call, waving as I try to work out which girl I'm addressing.

Ah! Now I see it—this is Heather Charles. She's got that stupid fairy tattoo on the inside of her wrist. *Oooh, if Heather Erickson sees it, she'll rip her a new one.* None of the Heathers are supposed to have anything that distinguishes them except the one accessory chosen that day. Today's clue is ponytail ribbons—they all have their color added to their carbon copy hairstyles.

Sometimes, it's easier to call them Heather Purple, Heather Gold, Heather Pink, and Heather Silver.

"It's about *time*," Heather Erickson snipes as she adjusts her gold ribbon, although it's perfect. "We've been waiting for*ever*. You know people wait for us, not the other way around, DD."

It takes everything inside of me to control my irritation. She knows my parents won't allow me to get a driver's license because they feel driving is 'beneath those of our stature'. Since I'm unable to escort myself, I'm at the whims of my drunken asshole parents for every event. I can't control how long Lucille and Bruno make me stand at attention so that they can remind me how little they care whether I'm happy.

"Apologies. My parents did the whole 'stand and be counted' BS again, and I thought Lucille was going to drone on forever. As usual, Bruno milked every second of flexing his uber tiny dick powers before he sent me running along with his pet psycho." I hitch my thumb over my shoulder, showing the bulky Komodo hovering about a hundred feet back. I don't have to look to know he's there; I can *feel* his menacing sneer in my bones.

Sniffing, Gold shrugs and turns on her heel. "Figure it out next time, DD, or we'll leave you behind. Managing the egg and sperm donors is part of being a Council heir. If you can't hack it, they'll eat you alive."

I blink, tilting my head at her for a moment. The Heathers have always been bitchy, but something in Gold's attitude today smacks of unearned entitlement. I have no fucking *clue* what flew up her ass and laid eggs, but her lemon sucking bullshit is going to piss me off today. I've had enough of people acting like they own me, and she's pushing that button hard. "Where are we going first, guys?"

A change of subject should distract them—they're not too bright.

Baring her teeth, Gold gives me a knowing look. I guess she caught my lack of groveling. "We are meeting up with Todd, Chaz, Brett, and Brad on the quad. They assigned us a tour guide, but we're going to ditch them as soon as possible."

"Yeah!" Heather Charles pipes up as she tightens her silver bow. "E says we're going to find some hot college preds to invite us to a better afterparty for prom night."

My eyes narrow. College parties are typically 'emerged animals only'. No one wants to be the older student who makes a younger pred's animal emerge and risk the animal imprinting on them during a one-night stand. It fucking happens, and I've seen girls at our school absolutely lose the plot when the guy or girl who busted their fang cherry ditches them. It's like a baby duck without a mama—they wander around aimlessly.

They get very desperate, and it's fucking sad what trauma they put themselves through to chase that feeling. I have zero interest in drinking, screwing, and fucking up my life worse than it already is at a college party.

Besides, I have plans of my own, and they don't involve keg stands.

"You don't look excited," Heather Barrington interjects. Her tiny eyes glitter behind the colored frames of her oh-so-fashionable oversized frames that coordinate perfectly with her pink ribbon. "Don't you want to find the best prospects here before we walk through the doors? Who you know is everything at Apex. We plan to be at the top of the food chain, and anyone who gets in our way…"

All four Heathers smirk in a way that makes my blood run cold.

I've seen what those four can do to someone they consider 'beneath them' at Shifter Secondary. I didn't take part in the festivities, but I did nothing to stop them, either. My parents would have gone crazy if they'd gotten wind of me showing 'weakness', and that would have been the end of my bit of freedom.

It doesn't make me a good person, I know, but I didn't have a choice.

I'm especially glad I kept my big mouth shut now that Bruno is comfortably slinging death threats around.

"I don't want Lucille and Bruno to flip their switches if we get busted at a college party, that's all. You know how they are."

Heather Hopewell nods, studying me as the purple ribbon in her hair flutters in the breeze. "That's fair. Their edicts have always limited you."

That sounds sweet, right?

It's not. That's her backhanded way of saying I'm too cowardly to stand up to my parents. None of the Heathers are nice, and all of them are self-serving. I don't normally get this much ire aimed at me, though, and I'm curious why this morning they're all set on treating me like shit.

Did someone marry another Jonas Brother or something?

Forcing a smile, I tilt my head. "Shall we go inside and figure out what crusty old bat they're going to assign us for the tour, ladies?"

Gold sniffs, giving me a once over before turning on her heel. A snap of her fingers has the rest of them scurrying to follow, and I sigh in relief. If the boys are inside, their presence will distract the Heathers, and I can lean on Todd. He's always there to soothe me when my parents or the Heathers get me ruffled.

That's why *my* prom night plans involve a hotel room, champagne, and an overdue surprise for the best boyfriend in the entire world.

* * *

"If you'll follow me, I'll take you past our award-winning library." The poor tour guide rambles on, although barely anyone is listening. "The Draconis Memorial Library has a collection of texts that are only rivaled by the Apex National Library in the capital. Donors and alumni from around the world apply to the waiting list to have their documents, family records, and tomes inspected for authenticity prior to our historian accepting them as part of collections. We have a state-of-the-art preservation room, and a climate controlled vault in the catacombs to help protect the eldest of our valuable acquisitions…"

"There hasn't been a worthy Draconis since that incident," Gold snarks. "Why do they keep the name?"

"Probably because the heirs throw so much money at the school, they can't turn them away. It's unfortunate that a shitty family like that gets to be part of the awesomeness of Apex," Todd laughs.

His high-pitched giggle sometimes makes me cringe, and his boys, Chaz, Brett, and Brad, join in immediately.

It's creepy how alike they are sometimes.

"Maybe the school figures that one person's mistake doesn't define an entire family?" I suggest, frowning at the joy they're taking in dragging people we don't even know. Everyone knows the Draconis family keeps to themselves since the 'incident', and no one really knows what kind of people their clan has now.

"Oh, sure! Some *loser* destroys valuable artifacts and stuff like a million years ago, and you want to throw them a pity party. Typical," Gold mutters, looking at the other girls. "DD and her bleeding heart."

Pink gives me a predatory grin. "That's what will get you one day, DD. Never help anyone. We're predators, and we eat the weak until we're at the top. That's the way of our world."

I roll my eyes. "The four of you give me a migraine when you get like this. You need to eat more. You're thin enough as it is."

They all whip their heads around to glare at me, and the boys giggle again. Chaz mutters something about a chick fight, and I look at Todd. He smirks at me, and I growl under my breath. He's a much less considerate boyfriend when the group of chuckling fools is tagging along. Fed up with their antics, I pull away from Todd's side.

"I'm going to the bathroom. Back in a few." The Heathers light up, clearly planning on moving as a unit, but I point at a large building on the map. "I think the gym is next on the tour. You might find college guys there."

Just like that, the entire group switches gears and makes a beeline for the gym. Nice to know they're worried about if I'll catch up.

Sighing, I rub my temples and head for the library bathroom to splash water on my face. On the way, I stop at a window, looking out at the small, enclosed courtyard that must be a break area of sorts for staff. I slip through the doorway and walk toward the tree at the courtyard's center. As I take a moment to admire the flowers, there's a noise from the window lining the exterior wall, and I squint my eyes to see what it might be.

Holy fucking shirtballs. Is that what I think it is?

HOT FOR TEACHER

Fitz

Aubrey will flambé us if we get caught in here again, but it's near the end of the semester and the brats at this bloody hell-hole are too busy avoiding their heat cycle or planning graduation parties to notice what the staff are doing. I wouldn't care if they did; it's my right to enjoy my consort anytime I please. However, dodging pissed off dragon fire is never on my list of things I want to do, so I check my watch.

As long as Chess arrives soon, we'll have time before the giant prick gets back from the safety committee meeting.

As if I summoned him, Chess appears in the doorway, shutting it behind him and clicking the lock. His adorable floppy curls make me smile and he pushes up thin silver wire glasses as he rushes over to me. I grab his face between my hands and plunge my tongue into his mouth without preamble. His rumbling purr kicks in immediately, and my entire body shivers. It's really not fair that he's able to do that and I'm not, but since he's mine, I'll let it slide.

"*Dépêche, mon amour*[1]," I growl as our lips break. "Aubrey will be back from his meeting in exactly… fifteen minutes."

My lover drops to his knees with a smirk, his sparkling amber eyes mischievous. "That sounds like a challenge, Fitzy."

I open my mouth to respond, but he's already pulling my cock out and sliding his warm lips over it. My eyes slam shut as Chess takes me down to the back of his throat without pause, his thumbs resting on the notches at the top of my hips. Groaning as his tongue lengthens and wraps around me with every quick bob, my hands scramble to hold on to the edge of the nearby bookshelf.

My darling boy takes great pride in his ability to make me lose the tight control I have over myself most of the time and I adore allowing him to do so.

Lifting one hand off the shelf, I bury it in his sandy curls as he suckles and scrapes his teeth over me exactly how I like it. "Fuck, baby, you weren't kidding," I pant softly. "Such a good fucking boy."

Chess hums his pleasure at the praise, flicking his tongue over the piercing on my tip, and I shudder. He knows what that means and speeds up, meeting my thrusts with his mouth as I fuck his face harder and harder. His fangs descend, catching tender skin, and that throws me over the edge with a shout. Cum spurts into his mouth and his agile feline tongue catches every drop until I stop moving, wilting against the surface of the bookcase with a growl.

When he releases me with a pop of sound, I jerk him up, kissing him hungrily as the taste of me dances on my tongue. I shift my eyes to the icy blue of my tiger as we pull apart and his cheetah looks back at me with satisfaction. Our breaths are harsh in the quiet stacks until he finally gives me a lopsided grin. I grin back, chuckling as he zips me up carefully, straightening my vest and tie.

"Aubrey will murder us if he scents this again," he whispers, his expression playful. "I'd beg you to fuck me over that table if you couldn't set your clock by his damn schedule."

"I'd do it if I thought we'd get away with it. You're owed a treat for that performance." Leaning in, I kiss his lips lightly before I tilt my head curiously. "Alas, we're limited by our exile in this ridiculous place and our friend's anal retentive tendencies."

His smile fades a little, and he sighs. "It will never stop being bullshit that your family sent Felix packing, because he refused to give up his consort after he was engaged. Everything I researched said most ambushes allow for poly groups, especially if it's their Raj."

I shrug, waving my hand dismissively. "My father has always been a royal prick, even before he took the Bloodstone throne. Once our elders brokered the deal with the Council when Felix and I were pups, he stopped running our land according to tiger traditions. Instead, he looked to expand operations worldwide, and that means he's had plans for a political marriage for Felix since we popped out of our mother."

"At least he appreciates the sacrifice you made to come with him. I doubt any of your cousins would do the same for their siblings," Chess says softly.

I arch a brow at him. "You came with us as well, but Felix's consort declined. That's the real salt in the wound. My twin gave up his throne for a woman who curbed him as soon as he was no longer the heir apparent."

"As if I was staying there without you." My lover looks at me seriously, a sadness in his eyes that I wish I could assuage. "I'm an adopted spare, Fitz. They would have killed me when we were cubs if you hadn't taken a shine to me. We both know your father only put up with us because you weren't in line for the throne."

He's right. Our ambush adopted Chess when his diplomat parents went missing on a jungle tour of our isle. My parents claimed they took him because they felt responsible for our guards' carelessness in defending the visiting ambassador and his wife, but I've always doubted that was true.

Even my mother is as cunning as they come, and being able to parade their charitable endeavor around in public with their sons has always been their modus operandi. To the court at Bloodstone, Chess is a reminder to outsiders that we may be in business with the Council, but we will not bend a knee to their demands. After all, his parents were there to inspect the treatment of the imprisoned predators sent to our 'reform' school, and my family didn't want word of what actually goes on there to leave the island.

It wouldn't do for the public to know what happens to the children and teens who live there when they misbehave.

"You and Felix weren't in a place to stop any of it yet, Fitz. You know that in your heart."

Chess' words pull me out of my morbid musings and I nod. "I know. We couldn't stop that anymore than we could change the rites of passage or the ambush trials. We lost so many cubs to those."

Something moves, catching the instincts of my predator and I spin, holding my boy close to me as I let my cat's eyes observe the courtyard just beyond the large window next to us. Something deep in my gut unfurls as I watch a gorgeous blond girl wander over the soft grass as she studies the immense tree growing there. She pauses for a moment to read the plaque on the sculpture next to it, then bends to examine the lush flowers planted at its base. Her position flashes the tops of creamy thighs barely covered by an academy skirt and I suck in a breath as my dick jumps in my pants.

"What are you looking at?" Chess hisses as he struggles to get out of my kung-fu grip. I turn him around, letting him feast his eyes on the luscious treat flashing us glimpses of white that are likely her panties. "Ohhhhh, my."

Grinning ferally as my fangs drop, I rake them along the cords of his neck. "Oh, my is right. That girl is fucking stunning."

"I can feel that," he shoots back wryly and in retaliation, I grind against his ass until he moans softly. "Fuck, Fitz…"

My hand slips down to cup his crotch and I'm pleased to find him hard and ready. I know for a fact that Chess has never slept with a female before, and his interest in this one makes my cat prowl. Unlike my brother, I never put limitations on my consort; instead, I offered him a vast array of options from my plate, but he's never so much as blinked toward anyone but me. This development is unexpected and darkly fascinating at the same time. Since he deserves a reward for his prowess earlier, I unzip his chinos, pulling his cock out to stroke it as I pull him tight to my front. "Do you like her?"

A whimper is my only answer, but it tells me enough to continue working his thick shaft slowly. Our anonymous hot girl rights herself as I squeeze his balls, only to prance over to another section of flowers and put her pert ass in the air again. Chess makes a low yowling sound, then turns to rub his face on mine as he pants. He finds words when she wiggles a little, showing more of that enticing white lacy edge.

"She's statuesque like a pin up…" he says with a ragged sigh. "I could write poems about her and they would never do her justice."

Uh-oh. It aroused his muse as well.

"Do you want to compose or come, my darling?" I murmur. Sinking my teeth into his neck to hold him in place, I rumble darkly and move my hand faster on his dick.

"B-B-Both…," he gasps as he jerks in my palm and grinds back into my rock solid erection. "I want her… and you. Together."

My eyes pop open and if I weren't putting my consort in a submissive position, I'd let out a yelp of pure joy. Squeezing him again, I let my teeth pierce the skin slightly so he shudders hard and makes a whining sound that I know means he wants permission to come. I lick the small blood droplets on his skin before I mutter, "Just a little longer, *mon amour*. You're doing so well."

I look out at the girl as she walks around the courtyard. Something about the way she's specifically avoiding looking in this direction makes me wonder if she's scented or heard us. I'm uncertain if she's emerged or not, given I've never seen her before and I'd never forget those cherry red lips made for plundering. She pauses, lifting her head to look up to the sky, before she approaches the tree and leans against it as she slides to the ground.

I'll be damned if we don't have an unobstructed view of those lacy scraps she's wearing now that she's sitting.

"Fitz… please…" Chess groans and his cock pulses in my palm. I know his eyes are glued to this reincarnation of Botticelli's Venus, as much as mine are. "Would you let me fuck her? With you?"

My cock is going to burst through my damn pants at this point. I should have fucked him earlier and given the book dragon the finger if he caught us. "Oh, baby, I'd *love* to make a kitty sandwich with you and this angel."

His hips buck into my hand now and I lick away some of the blood with a dark smile. When I lift my eyes to look at the girl, I notice she's squirming on the ground a bit and it looks as though she's watching us through her lashes.

I always wondered if that window was two-way glass and now I have my answer.

If the delectable shifter out there wants a show, she'll get one. I drop my other hand to knead Chess' balls while I continue stroking him, then nip my way up his jaw to take his mouth. Kissing him roughly, I work his cock and sac until I feel them tighten before I jerk my mouth away. My voice is a harsh whisper against his lips as I say, "You may come."

Just like that, his entire body tenses and his dick spurts all over my hand, gushing sticky fluid so hard that some splatters on the glass in front of us. His plaintive yowl calls to me and I curse virulently as a sudden orgasm hits me, making a mess of the inside of my favorite fucking suit. I'd punish him for it, but I can't bring myself to be even a bit displeased with the turn of events that just transpired.

"I'm sorry, Fitz," he says as he wilts against me. "The goddamned window."

Laughing softly, I place a soft kiss on his lips. "I'm not even mad, babe. That was fucking amazing."

Chess flushes with pleasure and straightens, moving out of my embrace to walk over to a small drawer where he stowed a pack of wipes for surprise clean ups at the beginning of the semester. I take them from him, dropping to gently clean him up and place a kiss on his dick before I tuck him away. Grimacing, I undo my slacks and do the same to myself, sighing as I realize I'm going to have to race over to the gym next door and steal a change of clothes from my locker before I head to the tech wing.

"I love a little afternoon delight, but this was next level." My cheetah gives me a shy smile as he looks out the window to see our peeping student sashay out of the courtyard. "I think she was touching herself while she watched."

"Damn," I whistle. "That's what I get for being obsessed with your dick. I missed it entirely."

"Maybe next time we won't?"

"Bet on it," I rumble. Winking at him, I head for the door, checking the hallway as I leave him staring into the empty court-yard with a look of wonder on his face.

As long as we don't get toasted by a cranky book hoarding dragon, I'm game.

Better Off Alone

Aubrey

Watching the annoying half of the tiger twins leave my library, I sigh. This is my world—my haven—and it riles the slumbering lizard inside every time he and Chess defile my study rooms. Not for *that* reason, thanks ever so. I could give a shit that two dudes are fucking; I'm more concerned about their use of my space as their personal knob gobbling spot.

It irks me for several reasons, including the lack of interest in reading or books in this hellhole of a school. The texts and tomes here are full of history, adventure, knowledge, and romance, but the spoiled brats that attend this place are only concerned with electronics.

Fucking Instagrowl or RipTok or whatever the bloody hell they're doing these days.

Grumbling under my breath as I use my badge to lock the elevator Felix exited in, I walk back to my desk. There's a million requests for archiving from the prominent families that I plan to ignore until summer break. There are a few carts of books that need to be re-shelved in the staff-only section, but that can wait. The email icon on my Smackbook is blinking, and if the number on it is accurate, I probably have a hundred password-reset requests from students and staff alike.

Whoever decided that hot-blooded predators with zero patience should use passwords with eight characters, a symbol, and a number didn't think very far ahead. Of course, given that the total of our current IT department is an over two thousand year old dragon and a fucking baby-faced ostrich shifter from Victim U, it's not surprising our system isn't predator friendly.

I shake my head. I've been at this place too damned long. I shouldn't use the student slang for Vassal University. Of all the staff here, Renard and I can remember when the delineation between pred and prey shifters wasn't as pronounced as it is now. Hell, we can remember when the two groups actually worked together to help our populations flourish together rather than relegating the prey shifters to the lower and working classes.

Betsy isn't a bad sort; she's just terrified of almost everyone here. The poor girl jumps at shadows all day long, and damn near has a panic attack if she has to leave her office to interact with anyone in person. As if being a prey animal assigned to work at *the* premier predator college in the nation isn't bad enough, she's a stick thin, frail nerd in horn-rimmed glasses with a high-pitched voice that commands zero authority.

I'm afraid for her safety—and rightfully so. A pack of coyote shifters tore apart the last IT guy last year, and the administration made sure Betsy knew about it when they brought her in. She's carried a whistle, a stun gun, and an emergency alarm pendant ever since she walked in the double doors of my domain.

Not that any of that would save her.

A loud buzzing emits from under a stack of admissions paperwork on my desk, and I growl this time. I despise my DiePhone with a fierce passion because it's constantly reminding me that no matter where I go, someone can bother me, even when I'm trying to focus. Plopping down in the throne specially crafted for when I want to let my wings out, I pick the cursed thing up and roll my eyes at the screen.

It's Fitz, asking *yet again* if I have an update on the same topic he prodded me about earlier in the day. He emailed me two hours ago, but my fellow outcast has the worst case of ADHD I've ever seen. That tiger can barely focus on more than screwing around and Chess for long enough to teach his classes, much less sit still for any lengthy explanation about historical tiger throne challenges.

That's why I sent him packing—I don't have a lot to divulge because the Bloodstone ambush is one of the more secretive shifter sects and what I have is a lot of tiny leads that will probably result in more questions.

Fitz doesn't have the patience to hear all of that, and I don't have the time to hold his hand. The mountain of work on my desk isn't getting smaller with the end of the semester drawing near, and they didn't assign me an aide to share the burden. My hyperactive friend doesn't understand that the staff members who don't spend their time teaching computer crime have actual work to do even when they don't have students in front of them.

Closing my eyes, I reach out with my senses, checking to make certain that the upstairs portion of the library is empty. Most shifters have one highly developed sense that aids in their pursuit of prey and defense against larger predators, but dragons are a rare breed, much like my gargoyle friend, Renard. Our species have existed long enough that our traditions predate modern shifter practices. We do not breed with other predator species, and typically keep to our clans, hidden by old magick from a time when shifters were not so wary of the existence of other supernatural beings. Gargoyles and dragons have much in common, and that we are both exiled from our clans is both unusual and unfortunate.

That's another reason I dislike Fitz and Chess turning my hideaway into a sausage salon—it reinforces the fact that I have no options for the pups a king should produce in this place. No dragons—unless they get exiled—will ever come to Apex Academy, and even if I was inclined to thumb my snout at the rules of my people, I have issues keeping books safe from my fire. I can't risk getting intimate with a female pred because I can't accidentally fry someone and get sacked by the Headmistress or, worse, sent to Bloodstone Isle for killing one of the Council's darling heirs.

The fire in my belly sparks in frustration at my situation, and I snort, blowing a few smoke rings as I try to calm my dragon. He doesn't like that I don't let him be free very often. I need to prevent a repeat of the 'incident' that caused my isolation, and I spend an inordinate amount of time soothing him, particularly when I get upset.

I've read every book ever written about controlling your beasts, taken advanced shifting classes from Felix, and lately, I even moved to reading anger management books written by *prey*, of all things.

Almost nothing calms the grumpy asshole inside of me, and his irritation always makes mine worse.

Once I've verified that the area is deserted, I use my stupid phone for one of the few functions that I appreciate it for: music. The sounds of EDM fill the space around me and I close my eyes. I've never been able to figure out why this electronic shit soothes my inner beast, but it does. I discovered the surprising effect in the nineties, and once I did, I learned everything I could about the culture.

Sue me, I'm a goddamned librarian, and I can't help myself.

A hint of a smile graces my lips for the first time today, and I lean into my desk. Taking out a selection of the calming trinkets I keep there, I place them around my workspace. The fuzzy pens, small stuffed unicorn, and springy bobble heads help me keep the lizard zen so I can actually work on the summary I need to send Fitz before he pings my phone every five minutes until I answer. I know from experience that I have little time to compose it before that happens, so getting my horns in the game is essential.

I yank my desk closer, opening my P-Mail and ignoring all the messages to start a new one to the tiger, using lingo that will make sense to him to help get his attention.

Calm the fuck down, bro.

I haven't found new texts to examine this week. I know you're anxious to find a loophole to allow Felix to take his rightful place as Raj. I would have been the Dragon King centuries ago if not for my fuckup, so I get why you're so hyped up.

However, your family is almost as bad as R's or mine with keeping mum about laws and rituals outside of the family. It might be worse because running Bloodstone means they're feared by predators who are afraid to speculate publicly.

I found a few anonymous sources on the prey-net by creating new credentials to impersonate one of them. I'm slowly working my way into their groups and servers. It is much more likely that the lower animals will gossip about 'horror' stories of our kind than preds will risk getting caught talking about the founding families.

If I have to go much deeper into their system, though, I will require your help. My skills do not extend to the hacker level, and if I must use tech to locate information, it may require those gifts. I believe the weasel families are all involved in the development of the Smackbook empire—there has to be a black sheep in the family who refused to be enslaved by the Ericksons' company who will be useful in obtaining bits of their coding.

I will help you, but you must learn to be patient.

DO NOT FOLLOW UP WITH FIFTY TEXTS, FITZ, I HAVE WORK TO DO.

OF COURSE, I KNOW THAT'S A FUTILE REQUEST WHEN I HIT 'SEND', but it never hurts to try. Sliding my phone into the pocket of my blazer, I look at the piles of work, pondering which inane task to do first.

The immediate ding of my D-phone makes my dragon snarl again, and I snatch the bunny rabbit stress ball. Squeezing it as I gnash my teeth, I ignore the next few dings while I count my breaths in Greek. As they escalate, I switch to Persian, and still they persist. When the rapid fire texting stops for a moment, I sigh in relief, picking up my coffee mug from the warmer at the front of my desk. I'm about to sip when the ringer goes off, the 'Pretty Fly for a Cat Guy' tone making me hurl the mug across the room. With a roar of irritation, I stand, looking down at the completely ruined bunny ball in my other hand.

Damnit, Fitz, that was my favorite!

I abandon the mess, stalking out of my office mid-shift. My wings get stuck in the frame even though it's been widened for me, and another roar escapes, rattling the window panes in the library. I can't lose control here—not in this place, not again. Forcing the wings to flatten to my back, I slam the door behind me, listening for the lock to click into place. When it does, I jump over the edge of the balcony, landing in the middle of a table with a crack.

Fuck. Now I'm going to have to replace that bloody thing this week.

The phone is still ringing in my pocket as I charge through the double doors at the front of the library and head to the courtyard. My wings lift and spread, my clawed feet push off the ground, and I take to the air in my half-shifted form, heading for the clock tower. Fitz will either be there dicking around on the Slaystation with Chess, or he'll go there when he finishes whatever the hell it is he actually does between classes besides defiling my library.

Either way, that asshole is paying to replace this outfit *and* my bunny. Otherwise, I'm throwing his annoying ass off the Tower to see if pigs really do fly.

A Million Dreams

Exiting the bathroom, I place my hands on my cheeks, feeling the skin burning under my touch. The flush won't go away, no matter how many times I dabbed my neck or face to cool down. I'm not any different from any other teen—I have my moments and this was clearly one of them. Sitting under that tree and watching the gorgeous men in that room might sound a little creepy, but I can't explain why I couldn't take my eyes off of them other than an excess of 'horny-mones.'

Kill me now.

I'm so flustered that I used Gold's stupid nickname for a bodily function. I swear, if you're not careful, being friends with them is like slowly being assimilated with the Kardashian sect of the Borg. Their culture seeps into your vocabulary, tastes, and mind before you even realize it's there.

The whole 'sexual overdrive' thing is definitely my fault. I've steadfastly refused to use losing my virginity to force my animal to emerge, and because of that, it's made it hard for me to decide when it's actually right for Todd and me to take that step. He's been patient, but that won't last for much longer. His birthday is on prom night, and once we're both eighteen, it'll be more diffi-cult to resist the siren call of physical intimacy.

Plus, he's a male teenage shifter. Their urge to claim a mate gets stronger once they turn eighteen as a biological imperative, and though I believe we are mates, the families won't stand for us holding out much longer.

I know for damn sure that Bruno will get involved if we don't.

Taking another deep breath, I try to steady myself. The Heathers and the boys headed for the gym to sign up for their fitness elec-tive and mingle with the jocks. I'm less thrilled about joining them because I have zero intention of scouting college guys, nor do I think they'll offer dance here, so I'm going to worry about that later. Maybe I'll get lucky and they'll have something less... violent than sports next semester. Since I'm on my own and trying to get my heart rate to slow down, maybe I'll go towards the arts and humanities building.

If I'm lucky, an English teacher might be available to discuss my options.

My fingers rifle through the blood red and black folder they gave us at the start of the tour, and I sigh in relief when I pull out the map of the grounds. It's printed like an old style Gothic map and it makes me giggle. Of course, Apex wouldn't have a younger graphic designer do a fancy enhanced map with digital rendering and fancy photos—no, this school is all about tradition and the old ways.

That's why we have a map that looks like it's straight out of the Shire, and it's hysterical.

I mean, it's not like they couldn't afford to go on Fanger and hire someone.

With a shake of my head, I note that the library is close to the building I'm looking for. I slip the folder into my purse and slide my Bottega Veneta cat-eyed sunglasses on. The doors of the giant atrium at the front of the library automatically open and I groan as a burst of hot air washes over me. Shifter Secondary would pick the hottest day of the month to tour a school that separates their buildings with football field sized spaces. I venture forth, map clutched in hand, as I head south towards the ornate building at the other end of the lake.

Luckily, no one can see me watching the water shifters have a class through my tinted frames. I'm truly hoping that my animal doesn't emerge as part of that class. It's possible, given the Drew lineage from Bruno—he's a croc and his father was a shark, but I have no interest in having to learn gills or whatever the hell else the amphibians, reptiles, and other water preds have to learn at first. There's a school of orcas leaping over the horizon, and I wonder how Apex divides the fresh and saltwater shifters.

Wrinkling my nose at the map, I notice that there's a second, smaller body of water near the dorms. That must be where the freshwater shifters wet their flippers. It occurs to me that despite Todd's family lineage of land preds, there could be water-based species that are recessive. He could turn out as something gross and slimy—that's a horrifying thought. I can definitely get behind a bear or a tiger, but I draw the line at breeding with a fucking fish.

Hera, help me... I just can't fathom it.

I shake my head to ward off the chills associated with imagining Todd or me emerging as non-land dwellers.

A glance at the map distracts me again when I notice that there's a clearing specifically marked as a Khan Training Area. That's where I'll hope we end up on this tour. I don't know what kind of teacher they have here, but the one at Shifter Secondary was pretty laid back. If someone emerged early but couldn't transfer to Apex, the bear shifter in charge of P.E. would switch their fitness elective to beginning shifter training with our resident counselor, Arwen. She's the luna of the Zion pack and loves working with new shifters.

Something tells me we won't get a professor with a gentle touch here, though.

I approach the arts and humanities building, tilting my head to gaze up at it. It's in a completely different architecture style than the rest of the academy. It almost looks as though someone with money upgraded the facilities, but insisted that the school build 'their vision' instead of something that complimented the rest of the campus. Honestly, that's not a stretch, knowing the whims of the elite predators who make up the council and heads of state.

Opening the doors to the building, I chuckle to myself when I see the name of the benefactors. That explains everything about how this place looks without having to ask a single question. The Shirdal Convocation Arts and Humanities Complex is a cluster of round buildings surrounding a central tower that I guarantee the raptor preds use for their flight training. They might use the clock tower as well, but I didn't see anyone near it as I passed, so it may not be a student zone.

My father loathes the Shirdals, and I've never been allowed to associate with the lower avian preds. Every time he has to attend a council meeting that involves the Shirdal heir, he spends days growling at Matilda—although she's a hawk and not an eagle. Afterward, he rants about the Shirdals refusing to breed with the Leonidas pride after a rift between the families. That's why we don't have griffins in the States currently, and he feels they've lowered our standing internationally.

I don't have the patience or the interest to decipher his drunken predator breeding theories most of the time, so I don't know exactly what the big deal is.

Who cares if we don't have griffins? I sure as hell don't.

The cool air of the quiet foyer of the arts building is a welcome change from the oppressive heat outside, and I look around. There's a gigantic statue of an eagle tearing apart a prey animal in bronze in the center of the room. Twin sets of steps lead to the next floor, and behind the statue, there's an enormous set of cherry wood doors. I walk around the ugly sculpture, curious to see what the curved doors lead to.

Set into the marble above the doors is a sign I never expected to see at Apex Academy: Aziz Shirdal Memorial Theater. Blinking, I place my fingertips on the door hesitantly. I've always wanted to perform in a play or, even better, a musical. My parents refused to let me try out for anything in all my years of schooling, so it limited my singing to my hairbrush in the bathroom. I press my lips together, deciding that I'm not quite brave enough to see what's in there just yet.

I'll come back once I find the head of the English department. After all, it's not like it's going anywhere, right?

"THANK YOU, MRS. CORMAC. I WILL START THOSE BOOKS OVER the summer, so I'll be prepared."

The ancient shifter eyes me through her thick glasses, her disapproval obvious. I'm not sure if it's because I creatively altered my uniform, she dislikes larger predators, or she hates students, but she might be the rudest person I've met on campus. Shifters don't age at the same rate as humans, and many of us don't age at all until very close to death. However, the crusty head of the English department made certain to reassure me she's nowhere near death, and that any shenanigans in her classroom would result in being nicked deep enough with her spur that I'd spend several days in the infirmary while I writhed in pain.

I'd never met a fucking platypus shifter in my life, and I'm not sure I ever want to again. Thank Athena she didn't decide to show me any of her shifted forms. She must be a mean old witch to avoid any of the *much* bigger carnivores in this school deciding to eat her over a poor grade.

Sighing, I lean against a wall, wishing I could find *one* thing to help me believe I'll survive the four years at Apex Academy without my soul dying. Hateful old bats with no faith in my talent staff, my focus area—creative writing. My parents despise my love of books and writing, the Heathers and the boys think it's nerdy and useless, and I can't even get support at school.

I feel like I'll be very lonely at this stupid academy, and I hate it.

Suddenly, I remember the heavy cherry doors in the archway downstairs. The lure of doing something that will piss off all the people who think I'm a bubble headed dreamer is thrumming in my veins. I chew on a fingernail for a moment, thinking about how furious Lucille will be if I disobey her edict.

Is this modicum of rebellion worth the fallout when she finds out?

Yes. Yes, it is. I'm tired of being the perfect daughter, heir, girlfriend, friend… only to feel like I'm still on the outside looking in. Nothing I do is good enough, and I've spent far too long doing what they expected instead of what makes me happy.

Besides, I'm only peeking in to see if they have any sign-ups for fall tryouts. That's not exactly *Rebel Without A Cause* stuff, right?

I push off the wall, striding down the hallway towards the stairs at the front of the building. My heels clack on the steps as I scurry down them as quickly as possible. I have to do this before I lose my resolve. If I don't, I'll never take the first step. When I get to the bottom, I hurry around the overly graphic eagle statue with a grimace and stand in front of the doors.

Straightening my spine, I push them open and walk into the large, ornate theater space. My jaw drops as I take in the velvet curtain, polished proscenium, and cushy seats. This is a masterpiece of a house, one to rival the theaters on Broadway, and I'm almost giddy to see what backstage looks like. The Shirdal family must have donated an absolute shit ton of money to renovate this space, and I wonder if it even gets used to its full capabilities in a school like this.

As I walk closer, I make out three people standing up center, clearly having an intense discussion. I can't make out the words yet, but two appear to be students—a girl and a guy—and the guy is gesticulating wildly. He's one of the most frightening men I've ever seen, with almost every inch of his exposed skin covered in badly drawn tattoos and a jet-black mohawk tinged in green. His appearance alone would have sent me running in the other direction usually, except for how joyfully he's chatting with the girl next to him. She's the most unique shifter I've ever seen—all rich sepia toned skin, a colorful undercut, and an outfit that screams Blackcraft Cult from head to toe.

And the third shifter is… *oh no.*

Sweet baby Artemis, even the fates are conspiring against me. I have to get out of here before anyone sees me.

There is no way I can interact with the shifter I watched get railed within an inch of his life at the library. His blond curls are pulled back in a loose man-bun that is just messy enough to imply he'd recently rolled out of bed—or out of a roll in the hay. Pale skin practically glows under the stage lights and I can feel my gaze drawn to his hands—mesmerized as I watch him furiously take notes while the students talk.

I'd watched his expressive face, and the adorable silver glasses as he writhed in pleasure. His lover was taller, with long dark hair that fell over his shoulders as he held onto the smaller man. They were both so goddess blessed hot I couldn't help myself, and now… I hope they couldn't see me, but I can't face him after seeing them like that. I just got my blood pressure backdown and now my heart is trying to leap out of my rib cage. I slowly back away from the stage.

"Hey! Blondie!"

My eyes must be as wide as prey as I turn to answer the shout from the curvy girl with the bright purple hair and tattoos. I can't force words out of my mouth, so I just point at myself like a blithering idiot. She rolls her eyes, nodding as she crooks a finger at me. Numbly, I walk down center, trying to ignore the flush that I can feel creeping up my spine to my face.

When I halt in front of the stage, the students look at me, clearly waiting for something. All I can do is stare at the hot blond, imagining myself sandwiched between him and his sexy top as sweat drips from our bodies.

Oh, my fucking gods, what is wrong *with me today?*

Pressing my thighs together, I pray that the other two shifters on stage haven't had their animals emerge yet, because I know I'm dripping pheromones and arousal everywhere.

I don't know if my life could get worse, but based on today, I doubt it.

"What's your name, sweet cheeks?"

I look at the mohawked, tattooed student for a moment with my mouth open before I croak out, "Delores. But my friends call me DD."

Don't Stand So Close To Me

Chess

My eyes widen as the siren that enchanted Fitz and me responds, standing not twenty feet away in the second row of the orchestra. Now that she's closer, I can see that her eyes are a brilliant cerulean color and the skin that appeared porcelain has a light peachy tone to it that makes my mouth water.

My hands grip the clipboard I'm holding hard enough to snap it, and I have to take a deep breath to find my center. Women have attracted me before, and Fitz has told me plenty about his exploits, but this is the first time I feel the need to experience it myself. Fitzgerald Khan has been my entire world since I was an orphaned cub and I simply found no one who made me feel the same way as him.

Until now.

Blood is rushing through my veins, roaring in my ears as I look at the lovely girl who played with us earlier. She's obviously a little embarrassed to see me and since I have no idea if she realized we could see her as well as she saw us, I can't exactly comfort her as my cat is urging me to. Instead, I lick my lips and walk to the lip of the stage. "This is a closed rehearsal. Are you a new student or part of the Shifter Secondary tour?"

I'd been so worked up by the time I got up the courage to slink past the dragon's office to my next class that I had to ask around to find out what might bring an unknown goddess to our campus at this time of year. If I read any of the stupid memos our flappy Headmistress sent out, I would have known, but Aubrey is one of the few professors I associate with who even attempts to keep track of all the shit she sends out. Ironically, I would have left the library knowing the score if Fitz and I hadn't been defiling his sci-fi section, but at least I found out before she showed up in the theater.

"Uhhhh…" She dips her head and looks sad as she mumbles something under her breath.

The animal inside of me strains at the look on her face, and I swallow hard. *Shit.* I definitely can't handle this if my cat is furious with me for making her look upset. I look at the students on the stage for help, but both of my stars just give me innocent looks. Before she takes off running, I blurt out, "If you're with the Secondary tour, I think they're at the gym going over the physical education electives for the fall with Professor Khan."

"Yeah." Her face reddens again, and she's quick to add, "I mean, I know, but I really wanted to check out some arts programs, so I came to the theater, and it was open…"

I'm saved by the tattooed gangster that comprises exactly half of my serious theater students. We have a top-notch facility at Apex and a few extremely talented exiles who are professors, but the arts aren't a favored major of the rich preds who attend this school. That's how I ended up being made head of the Theater Department despite my decided *lack* of credentials to back that title up.

Luckily for me, the dance and singing programs have specific professors, so I only have to manage the technical aspects of performances. I'm a fair hand at scripts and text, but I depend on Rufus and his best friend, Cori, to do the lion's share of the production work. I would have been much more suited to the English department, but those positions won't open until one of the old crones or our ancient friend, Renard, kicks the bucket.

People don't get exiled to Apex for a brief spell; once you're here, it's for life.

"Stay put, sweet cheeks!" The honey badger yells from his spot near the piano.

I watch as the adorable girl gapes at his rough exterior as he strides to the proscenium. It's hard to blame her—Rufus is one of those shifters who looks exactly like you'd expect them to once you realize what business their family is in. Though he's not actively part of the Pred-stasy empire now, Rufus, the gritty looking punk rocker who adores musical theater, was raised there. She wouldn't be allowed to hang out with him at home, but that might change if she comes here.

Even I have trouble saying no to Rufus.

"Walk towards us," the badger says, jerking his head at his friend. "I want to see something."

My cat wants me to interject, but I know Rufus isn't ogling her. He's definitely not being a creeper; Rufus has a much celebrated reputation for dating every guy on campus who will let him. The angel looks unsure for a moment, but steps into the aisle and does a quick catwalk back and forth for him. I see the wheels turning in his head as he watches her glide over the carpet and when Cori nods, he grins toothily.

"You're a dancer. I can tell by how you move. So if you want to skip out on the testosterone fueled circle jerk at the gym, you're welcome here. We have drama and dick, but we could sure as fuck use a choreographer."

Cori rolls her eyes at the overly gruff badger. "You're so full of shit, Ru-Ru. If you thought there were jocks jerking *anything* at the gym, we'd be looking at a trail of smoke as you took off."

That makes me smirk a little because the polar bear is right. She shakes her purple hair—this month's color—and sighs as if she should get a medal for putting up with all of us. "I, of course, have no such interest in man meat. But I'm down with you staying to watch or ask questions."

Talk about a proud teacher moment.

"Yes, Coco prefers the tah-co. Thank you, dear." Rufus runs his hand through his black and neon green hair as he chews on his lip ring and studies Delores again. "I think you should join us and see what fun the small but mighty theater department is at Apex."

That seems to shock her, but her apprehension turns to a shy smile as she walks to the stairs on the side of the stage to do as he suggested. I can't help but grin when she walks across the boards with more confidence now that my motley students have invited her, and I almost put my hand to my heart in an emotional, albeit dramatic, gesture. Her eyes flick to me and when she sees my encouraging expression, her face lights up like the sun is shining on her.

Do not start spouting poetry, Chess. You'll freak her out.

But her hair is like spun gold…

When I finally check back into reality, Rufus is talking animatedly, his hands waving as he points to different parts of the theater and I have to wonder how long I've been composing couplets in my mind. I catch him eyeing me as she responds to his questions and I wince—he can probably smell the arousal coming off me like a dead fish in the middle of the room. He grins wickedly, winking before he taps a finger against his lips. "DD, I think you should take a tour of the *entire* arts building while you're here. Fine Arts isn't a popular major because most of the snooty snoots won't let their kids do anything but prepare to marry rich or run their empires, but the Shirdals spared no expense when they paid for these facilities. I'll bet our favorite professor here would just *love* to show you all the nooks and crannies in this place. He's such a supportive faculty advisor; I *know* he'll make time for you."

I might not be the biggest pred, but I grew up on Bloodstone, so I know when someone is baiting me.

Clearing my throat, I give him a stern look. I ignore his and Cori's consistent dress code violations and let them operate with very little oversight, and *this* is how he repays me? That little shit is going to pay for this once I think of an appropriate punishment. Of course, he won't care—Rufus loves to stir the pot, and he enjoys watching people squirm even more. When I turn back to Delores—excuse me, DD—she's looking at me with wide, expectant eyes. Between inhaling her scent unconsciously, like a fucking creeper, and plotting my revenge on my meddling diva, I haven't responded.

"Yes. I could… definitely do that," I say lamely, avoiding glancing at the two would-be matchmakers, who are no doubt grinning like fools. "Follow me."

The angel dips her head, nodding at me as she walks behind me quietly. The silence is oppressive as we walk through the wings and down the hallway that runs alongside the orchestra level. When we reach the double doors to exit into the main hallway, I look over at her curiously. "DD, huh?"

Merciful Apollo, I'm never this awkward. I'm the nice one, for fuck's sake.

Her eyes crinkle at the corners, and she gives me that shy look again. "That's what my friends call me. My real name is Delores Drew, so…"

Drew? You've got to be fucking kidding me.

"I go by Chess, but it's not my real name, either," I reply as we head up the curving staircase to the second floor. "Don't ask me to tell you what my full name is—I'm convinced my mother was high."

That makes her grin, and she makes a motion like she's zipping her lips. The twinkle in her eyes is absolutely adorable and I feel my cock stir again despite how thoroughly Fitz worked me over earlier. I have to look away before I say something stupid, like how her eyes are like tide pools in the Caribbean. I still can't believe that the one female I've taken an interest in since puberty found her way to my rehearsal after she watched my consort jack me off like a beast. It's like the Fates are conspiring against me.

Before I can make a monumental error in judgment, I realize we've reached my personal studio. She tilts her head, looking at me curiously, and I open the door for her. "This is where people can find me when I'm not teaching or in rehearsal. I dabble in a lot of hobbies, so when the former visual arts teacher passed, they let me settle in here. Unfortunately, I'm hopeless with drawing, but I enjoy pretending I can paint or throw pots. Working with my hands gives me time to write, too."

Delores steps inside tentatively, peeking at the various projects I have in progress. The pile of knitting makes her whirl around and look at me in surprise. "This is beautiful, Professor. Are you making this scarf for someone?"

I flush, knowing it's not the most masculine hobby, but the repetitive motions soothe me when I have one of my attacks. "My... The two other professors I grew up with had a lot of responsibilities back home—things I couldn't be part of. Their grandmother taught me to knit when I was not much more than a cub. It helps me relax."

"She did an excellent job. Whoever this is for will love it." Her fingers trail over the material as if coveting the softness, and then she looks at me with another megawatt smile.

I feel she's not actually reserved; she's simply terrified to do or say the wrong thing.

"Do you have hobbies or talents, Delores? I assume you ventured into our little corner of the world for a reason." My question makes her nervousness return, so I step closer, hoping to make her feel less on the spot. "Rufus seemed to think so."

"Uh… I… Well, like you said, the Council families don't really encourage the arts. So, even if I dabble a little, I haven't had any real training or anything." She licks her glossy lips, then drags the lower one through her teeth and it takes everything in me not to groan.

Inside, I'm warring between my cat wanting me to get closer to her alluring scent and the creative in me wanting to rage that the parents of these kids decide their lives from the moment they're born with no regard to what makes them happy. I know that I'm lucky Fitz's parents didn't leverage me as a political tool as well, but my status as a smaller pred helped me stay under the radar. The parents of this girl, belonging to one of the most powerful families in the Council, have probably crushed her non-business related passions at a young age according to the rumors about her mother.

She's unemerged, too, so she can't fight back.

That's a guess based on her not noticing the arousal practically leaking from my pores as I watch her examine all of my secret projects. Her eyes meet mine again and I curse internally when I see the fear of rejection shining in them. This girl desperately needs someone to be in her corner. "Hypothetical question: if you could do anything you wanted for the rest of your life with no obstacles, what would it be?"

"Be on stage, performing things I wrote and choreographed for people who love seeing me."

Her answer is so quick that I know it's the truth. Her expression is so wistful—it reminds me of paintings where the women are full of longing for something off canvas. Delores Drew has a secret passion, and they have convinced her it's worthless, so she won't even admit she loves it when asked. Her plight makes my heart ache, but the one salvation I see is the interest Rufus and Cori took in her. That snarky asshole knew by looking at her she was hiding a talent and he encouraged her in a way that didn't seem insincere.

They're not wrong when they say psychopaths have a talent for identifying their prey.

Luckily, this particular nutjob has a soft heart for the people he collects and he's already decided he likes Delores. If she comes here in the Fall, he will probably adopt her immediately despite being a lower class than him. I try not to think about how that will open the door for Fitz and me to approach her, maybe even give her the support she desperately needs. My brain conjures up images of her in unique positions with us, and I almost miss her picking up the journal on the desk.

"Oh! This poem…" She looks up at me with wide eyes as she waves the book. "It's on the plaque in the courtyard. I saw it earlier…" Her cheeks flush with a delightful rose color when she realizes she's just admitted to being in a place she didn't belong, watching something she shouldn't have.

I know she's wondering if we noticed her and it makes my cheetah stretch out, purring with pride. My animal isn't ashamed of being submissive to Fitz; he enjoys taking care of our consort and being praised for our efforts. However, with Delores, he seems to know she's more prey than pred. I feel my eyes bleed amber and I close the distance between us. A rumbling growl echoes out of my mouth as I back her into the worktable, caging her in with my arms.

"Naughty girl. You were watching, weren't you? Did you enjoy the show, angel?" I grip the table to ensure I don't actually touch her, but my cat is pushing under my skin as I inhale the sweet scent of honeysuckle and jasmine.

Bast in a basket. I want to rub myself all over her until she's covered in my musk.

To her credit, she doesn't shrink away. Despite not having contact with whatever animal she has, she doesn't cower under the gaze of mine. Her clear blue eyes are hooded with desire that I can smell as she lets me corner her. Shaking my head, I spin away, raking a hand through my hair and I draw in shaky breaths. This is so unlike me—I never get this unreasonable about Fitz, though my cat certainly would like me to.

"I'm… sorry," I mutter with my back to her. "That was very rude and quite inappropriate. I understand if you need to file a complaint or want me to call Rufus…"

"No!" she practically shouts. I turn to look at her in confusion and her eyes drop to her shoes. "It's okay. I'm not upset, Professor."

Closing my eyes, I have to fight off a smirk. The teacher-student thing isn't my kink nor Fitz's, but I know a few people who are into it. Apex doesn't forbid having a relationship with consenting adult students, though it doesn't happen as often as you'd expect.

Undergrads who live on campus and have powerful families who could make our exiles infinitely worse than teaching here keep most of the staff from dipping their wicks in the pool very often. The possibility that the younger preds here might not have emerged yet when they arrive and could imprint on us is also a worry—one that would likely end in death if a contract has promised the student to another rich brat in some sort of deal. Instead, the staff are uncommitted and extremely open to all the possibilities available in our little employee village on the far end of campus. Fitz has his choice of hookups when he's hungry for more, and if I indulged, I could as well.

Unfortunately, this flowery scented recruit from a vicious elite family is the first person beside my consort I've reacted to.

I have to fix this *fast* before she changes her mind and tattles. "If your true love is performing, Rufus and Cori are your best allies."

"My true love…" she parrots in a thoughtful tone. It looks like the wheels in her head are turning and if nothing else, I know I've touched her in the way I'm *supposed* to, rather than the way I almost did. Looking up, she gives me a lopsided grin before she pushes away from the worktable. "Thank you, Professor. You've given me a lot to think about. I hope I see you again in the Fall."

Nodding, I let out a slow breath as she turns on her heel and heads out the door, leaving a trail of sweet floral scent behind her. My cheetah is pacing inside of me, irritated that I let her leave without marking her with our own scent, and my brain is screaming that we can't get involved with a student, especially one from her family.

The only thing I know for certain is Fitz and I are in deep shit the minute this girl moves onto campus.

Toxic

Delores

I don't look back as I run from the building like my skirt is on fire. The Professor told me to talk with the students from the theater, but I'm too embarrassed and turned on to face anyone. I take a sharp left, clutching my Vuitton to my shoulder as I scramble as far away from the Shirdal building as I can get before I run into any more hot-bod professors.

This is the long way around to the gym, but I couldn't care less. I *have* to put distance between me and the enticing Professor Chess. Between his body pressing up against mine and the show he put on with his boyfriend, I feel like my strings are being plucked but never played. I don't get what it is about those two that's got me melting like a snow-cone in the sweltering heat. Todd and I have fooled around tons of times, and *nothing* like this has ever happened.

Hell, if it did, I'm pretty sure that I wouldn't have been able to hold back on losing my V-card.

No, I know I've never felt like this before, even the time that Silver swiped the password to her older brother's PredHub account and we spent all night watching porn. It was a useful learning experience regarding other methods of calming my hormones, so it wasn't a complete write off.

Talk about things you have to hide in the least likely place that anyone in your nosy ass household would ever look—my vibrator is stashed where even the Council's investigators couldn't find it.

When I finally catch my breath, I notice that I've walked all the way around the building and past the large copse of trees surrounding the shifter training area. Shivering, I wrap my arms around myself. I shouldn't have wondered about my animal earlier. Without fail, worry about what pred I'll be and if it will please my father sends me into a panic spiral. I wish I could say that it won't matter, but deep in my bones, I know that isn't true.

If I'm not dominant in every way, Bruno is going to arrange for something horrible to happen to me; I just know it.

I stop for a moment, pulling the map out to study it. It wouldn't hurt to veer over and take a peek at where they will train us. Maybe it will ease my fears a little? That's not likely, but it's the excuse I used to assuage my curiosity about how Apex shifters master their forms.

As I approach the area delineated on the map, I hear loud noises coming from the clearing. They sound like grunts, snarls, and growls, but not the... kind I saw earlier. This sounds like fighting between several shifters. I pause, wondering if I'm asking for trouble by spying on whoever is having a lesson or one hell of a brawl. My foot lands on a branch, the soft crack making my entire frame tense—well, if they heard me, I'm screwed.

That's all there is to it.

My breathing resumes when I hear the battle sounds continue, and I creep forward to peek through the heavy bushes that fill the tree line. The fighting ring is an enormous carved stone with sigils and runes on it, and there are bleachers surrounding the circle, set up in the grass. They clearly use this as both a classroom and an arena, though I'm uncertain why they would need the second application here. On the opposite side of the clearing from me, I see a huge carved stone mountain that confirms this space as 'The Khan Ambush Battle Training Arena.'

I study the three shifters in the ring. Ignoring the forest for the trees, that's me every time. The earth shaking roars are coming from an enormous lion in half-shifted form—it's a female and a pretty aggressive one. Growls of frustration are escaping from a fully shifted black bear that seems to bide her time.

The most infuriated snarls are coming from the enormous orange Bengal tiger facing the two of them. He's fully shifted, his fangs stained with blood, and there are surface wounds dripping onto the stone beneath his massive paws. He's eyeing the bear, and I don't know enough about pred instincts to say for certain, but I think he's considering taking that one out of the fight first. The tiger throws his head back and roars into the sky, the sound both threatening and mournful at the same time.

I hope this school doesn't allow death matches onsite.

My father goes to that sort of thing on Thursday nights while Lucille is off banging her golf instructor—I mean, taking lessons. Neither of them know that I've followed them occasionally to see just what the hell they are up to and how it might affect me later on. I'll never forget the cage matches until the day I die. Those Khan thugs probably run that horror show, too. They use Death Island as a base for their operations, but their influence is felt all over the world.

A breath catches on my throat as the cat suddenly leaps at the bear, fiercely knocking the larger shifter to the ground. The lumbering bear bats its giant paws at the tiger, trying to knock it aside. Turning to look at the lion, I notice she's now fully shifted, prowling along the outer circle with narrowed eyes. She's looking for an opening, and if either of the two furry combatants on the ground give it to her, she'll strike. As if he can hear me thinking, the big feline lifts his head, snapping his jaws in the lioness's direction threateningly.

Seems like he wants her to wait her turn.

Something very troubling occurs to me and I put my hand on my chest. My heart is racing, and though I don't have an inner animal yet, I've heard stories about how preds frequently use fighting as foreplay. Did I just stumble upon another teacher hump session in progress? I barely made it through the last incident without embarrassing myself; I don't know if I can do that again. I mean, I assume its professors because students are clearly in class throughout the campus, and I'm uncertain if they're allowed to... co-mingle that way.

My thoughts flash back to the professor in the art room, and I close my eyes as I try to control my reaction. Even after being separated from both him and the location it took place in, I'm still transfixed by the memory of the intimacy and the reaction of my body.

Being a teenager sucks big hairy goat balls.

"Submit!"

The snarled command brings me back to reality, and I look over at the arena in shock. While I was reminiscing about my tryst, the tiger tapped the black bear out and is standing on top of the lioness. His massive paws hold her shoulders to the ground, and his dark eyes glare down at her as she... That does *not* look like struggling. Oh, that saucy minx is trying to use this battle to turn the cat on. The bear might be as well, because she's licking blood off her paw about as slowly as one can without looking like a goddamned psycho.

Scratch that, she definitely looks like a psycho—a big-assed furry bear psycho.

"Zhenga, I've told you more times than I care to count that I am no longer interested in your... kitty," the tiger says as he seamlessly transforms into a human again with a look of pure disgust. "Find someone new to lap your cream."

Frustrated roars echo out of both of the female shifters as they shift from animal to half-form to human. Their shifts are not even close to mastery like the large feline has, and they both pout while he pulls his clothes on. I'm also staring because I'm suddenly head to head with a man who looks eerily similar to the other half of the hottie duo I saw humping in the library.

I say head to head because his cock is so large it's practically poking me from where I'm hiding in the bush. Dragging my gaze above his waist, I realize he has to be related to Chess' dominating top. His thick, obsidian hair is cut short compared to the other man's long and wild hair, but they have the same square jaw, olive-toned skin, and dangerously dark eyes. They may even be twins, which, of course, sends a bolt of lust to my pussy like a road flare on the desperation highway.

I don't know what they're feeding the professors in the dining hall, but the Silver's family should package it and make another fortune off it. The diet the cooks are feeding these guys should be sold in bulk. Out of the three male professors I've seen today, no one isn't drool-worthy, and if I'm honest, the females aren't bad looking either. The only exception is my poison-wielding English chair and her cohort, the giant bulldog bat.

These chicks must teach something physically intensive. They're both much younger and clearly fitter than the geriatrics in the English department.

Using the angry snarling now emanating from the center of the ring as my cue to escape, I slip away from my hideout in the bushes. Heading east towards the lake, I tuck the map in my bag and prepare for the scolding Gold will give me for how long I've been gone.

Maybe I should have let the scary tiger dude catch me watching. I could use some lessons in self-defense.

HALFWAY AROUND THE BACK EDGE OF THE LAKE, I STOP TO PEER AT the water shifters in awe. I said I didn't want to emerge as one of them, and that is definitely true. However, no one can deny how beautiful the orcas look, leaping through the air as they chase one another. A pod of leopard seals is busy sunning themselves on the shore, and a herd of sea lions are making a fuss near the dock. Squinting, I walk closer to the edge of the lake, holding my hand up to shade my view more.

I'll be a mangy hyena shifter. If I hadn't seen this with my own eyes, I'd never have believed it to be true.

The dock has a small structure on it, and by the smell wafting along the breeze, I can only assume that it houses fish for the water shifters to eat. The sea lions are crowded around the edges of the dock, trying to wrangle food forcibly from the staff members that are distributing it. Unfortunately, they're prey animals, and though they are larger than normal, they are struggling with the aggressive herd.

That's not even the most amusing part.

The unlucky bastards are a band of fucking raccoons dressed as pirates. I'm not sure why in Hades they're dressed as pirates unless it's going along with the aquatic theme, but one of them is poking an angry bull with a sword to fend him off.

Who in the name of Poseidon thought letting prey animals feed preds was a good plan?

Before I can pull out my phone to call the main office for help, the sky goes dark as an enormous flying shifter literally blocks out the sun as it swoops down from above. I watch as the planks of the dock buckle with the weight of the winged warrior as he lands, his roar echoes off the hills, louder than any I've heard so far today. The herd of sea lions scatters so fast that you'd think the wrath of Zeus was about to rain down on them and perhaps it is.

I've never seen a pred that looks like this one. His skin is as dark as obsidian, and his eyes glow like the seas during a storm. His hair is flowing down his back, the raven tresses blowing in the breeze as it gusts over the water. He turns, his gaze sharp as he glares at the herd of sea lions cowering on the shore, and then his wings spread wide.

"What is this *nonsense* disturbing my peace in the Tower?" The beast roars again, revealing a mouth full of fangs as he looks around accusingly. "Who *dares* to threaten the Captain's crew? Have I not made it *clear* that they are under my *protection?*"

It's like time stops as every water shifter freezes in place. From the shiver of great whites to the leaping orca pods to the sunbathing seals, no one moves an inch or utters a single word. There's no place for me to hide, so I stand as motionless as possible, hoping that will keep his stormy eyes from landing on me. No one wants to incur the wrath of this monster.

"Renard, your most gracious gargoyle-ness, we are grateful for your protection," the raccoon wearing the captain's hat says as he salutes.

That's how quiet the lake is now—I can hear a raccoon supplicating to a gargoyle from across the water. It's more interesting than a pin dropping, that's for sure.

Waving his hand at the Captain dismissively, the gargoyle—*who knew they ever left their clan lands?*—strides over to the end of the dock and snarls. "If I hear of *one* student giving the crew trouble, I will ensure every predator involved will suffer so greatly they will wish I had simply drowned them. You have been *warned.*"

With that, the winged guardian pushes off the dock, taking flight with ease. His path curves towards the top of the tall clock tower, and I realize why the school placed one on the grounds. Gargoyles favor them, and some legends are apparently just as much fact as fiction.

I put my hand on my chest, feeling my heart beating rapidly again. For the fourth time today, I feel desire coursing through my veins like warm honey. I've got to get to the damned gym and find my friends. I adjust my sunglasses and start walking towards the Leonidas Gymnasium at a rapid clip.

Otherwise, I won't be held accountable for my actions when the next toxic alpha asshole crosses my path.

Girlfriend

They propped the doors to the gym open, and I breeze through them, marveling at the size of the structure. Everyone knows Leonidas Pride controls every major sporting outlet, athletic wear company, and runs all the competitive sports leagues both nationally and internationally. Their reach is almost as big as my parents', and definitely on par with the Ericksons and their tech.

It makes perfect sense that they'd build a professional grade tribute to themselves at the premier pred school in the country. From the mechanical bleachers to the shining basketball court in front of me to what smells like an Olympic sized pool hiding somewhere, this facility is beyond state-of-the art and *far* too nice for a school.

The boys are over at the back of the court getting chewed out by…

Oh, no—not again.

"I *cannot* catch a break today!" I mutter to myself as I scurry over to the gaggle of giggling Heathers.

If I'm lucky—which I probably won't be—I can hide behind my friends, so the buff guy I watched pound the adorably nerdy professor doesn't see me. The encounter in the art studio clarified that the watching was a two-way street, and I am not equipped to go head to head with the other half of that duo.

What the hell is he doing here?!

"DD, *where* have you *been*?" Gold grouses. "Just *look* at that spectacular specimen of man meat over there with the boys. He's been yelling at them for five minutes, and it's so *hot*."

A flush creeps up my neck because I absolutely know how hot this specimen is, and I refuse to tell the Heathers about my flirtation with voyeurism. I know they're my friends, but lately, they seem to shrug everything I tell them off like it's no big deal. Something in the power dynamic has shifted, and I don't know what it is.

I force a smile, knowing that Gold's tapping foot means she's getting impatient, waiting for my reply. "I went to tour the arts building while you guys came here. I got caught up talking with a professor."

That much is true, and it should be bland enough to keep Gold from questioning any further.

"You were gone an awfully long time," Purple remarks, her eyes narrowing as she studies me. "What could you possibly have talked about that would take that long?"

I'm fairly certain Purple can barely read, so it doesn't surprise me she's jumping to a conclusion with no facts. She's the most sniveling of all the Heathers, and the one whose family has the smallest empire. The Honeywells built their fortune off of flashy temples and televangelism—if it's religious and crooked, their hands are in the pot. I could easily call her Heather Hypocrite instead, but I'm mostly trying to keep out of sight until the deliciously sweaty hottie lets the boys off the hook.

It figures—with a body like that, of course, he'd be in the fucking gym at three p.m.

"You're turning red, DD," Pink chimes in. "I think H. has found a hole in your story. What were you *really* doing? Were you trying to lure buff college preds without *us*?"

The shrill shriek of her question causes the professor to dart his eyes towards us, and I crouch behind the Heathers, trying to stay hidden. I'd love to pop Pink right in her fat mouth, but I don't want to start a war—I just want to keep out of sight.

"No, I wasn't. I was in the library, then I walked to the arts building. It took a little time to find the English professors, and I talked to them for a bit. They're literally ancient. After that, I took the long way around the lake to the gym to meet you guys. That's it— no secret hot preds."

I'm a big lying liar, and I'm going to Hades for it. But I'll be damned if I'm going to encourage them to lust after the staff before we even matriculate to this place. Apparently, that's my job, and I'm not feeling generous today.

They all look at me for a moment. Heather E. shrugs, and I guess that ends the discussion. I peep over their shoulders, trying to see if the public spanking is going to end soon. It feels like it's been going on forever, but since I'm so fucking nervous, it's probably only been three minutes.

Gold catches me looking and smirks. "You've got Todd, DD. Let the rest of us flirt with the buff gym kitty. We're DTF and you're not."

I frown at her. "None of us are DTF. We haven't had our animals emerge, and we all know what happens when you screw around with older guys for your first time. That whole imprinting thing sounds like a nightmare. I'd hate to be stuck pining after a guy that was only looking for a one-night stand."

Pink looks at her nails, sighing to herself. "I suppose."

"If you say so," Purple chimes in.

Silver nods, her eyes darting to Gold as if trying to figure out what to say. "That sounds like a shitty deal."

Is she kidding me? A shitty deal? It's awful.

"Well, I think it's worse than we even know, and that's why I'm glad we've all waited for the right time to cross that line. Our parents thought they could push us, but we held firm, despite their threats, and now we'll all be able to share that moment with someone special."

A giggle escapes Gold as she continues to drool over the teacher. "Uh-huh. Well, at least you've got yours all planned out, DD. You and Todd, after prom? Bow-chicka-wow-wow…"

My eyes widen as the professor turns his head towards our group again, and I hiss, "E! I do not need random gym teachers to know about my sex life. Come on, all of you. I have to get back to the admissions building in time to meet Bruiser or I'll get busted. Let's go!"

I grab Silver's hand, tugging her along until the rest of them follow me out into the spring heat. When we get outside, I drop her wrist, letting her make a big fuss about how delicate her skin is and how much she'll bruise from my manhandling. She's such a drama queen—I didn't even grab her that hard. I don't know if it's an off day, or if we're growing apart, but my friends are making me feel more like a tag-a-long than a part of the clique.

As I follow them past the library and lake, I tune out their babble about rock stars and celebs, instead considering a part of what Gold said. Todd and I plan to take the next step after prom, and I've been itching to go dress shopping for weeks. Maybe when I get home, I'll ask if Matilda can take me to the Cambridge Mall to get everything sorted. I'm certain I made a good enough impression at Apex Academy—at least, while I was on the official tour—and Bruno should receive a glowing report.

That'll buy me some goodwill, right?

My thoughts stray from my sweet, safe boyfriend to the professors I've met or seen today. From the smoke show teacher to the knitting cutie to the enormous roaring gargoyle and the dominating tiger in the training ring, I'm not sure I could decide if someone asked me to. That's ridiculous, of course, because everyone knows shifters have one fated mate...you can't just steal the whole dessert cart because you're feeling greedy.

Can you?

Holding onto my folder, I smile a little at my feet at the thought of sharing and being shared. I could get behind that... or they could get behind me...

Oh, my Goddess, what is in the air *here?*

"Delores!"

My eyes widen as a pair of fingers snap in front of them. The angry expressions of Gold and the rest of our group tell me I've missed something important while I was off in sexy dreamland. "Y-yes?"

"I *said*, are you ready to go? The guys caught up to us five minutes ago, and you've been off in La-La-Land," Gold snarks.

"Um, yes. I am. I have everything I need. I'll just..." I walk over to Todd, kissing his lips lightly before I pull back. He arches his brow at me, and I have no idea what his expression means. "I'm sorry I've been so distant, everyone. I'm just worried about what Bruno and Lucille will do when I get home."

Pink rolls her eyes. "Grow a pair, DD, and tell them to fuck off. You're like a scared little prey animal when it comes to them."

"I'll consider it," I grit out, pretending not to want to smack her again. Looking out over the parking lot, I see Bruiser pulling up to the front of the admissions office in the Escalade. "Oh, look, there's my three hundred pound shadow. I gotta go, but I'll text you guys later!"

My friends all mutter less enthusiastically than I would have preferred, but I let it go as I run for the car. Bruiser won't hesitate to leave me behind and tell my dad some bullshit like I refused to come home. The Komodo-domo is a sadist, and like the rest of the staff who are loyal to my parents, he relishes when I get in trouble.

Hopping into the chilly SUV, I take one last look at the group of teens waiting for their drivers. They're all huddled close together as if sharing some secret. I have got to stop letting Lucille and Bruno make me paranoid. My friends are amazing, if not the most empathetic preds, and my boyfriend is perfect, unless he's with his friends.

I close my eyes and let my mind wander to the dreamy professors I saw today. I can't wait until I'm at Apex next year so I can get to know them better—in a totally professional, student-teacher way, of course. Because by then, I'll be mated with Todd, and I doubt these older men would have an interest in me anyway... not that I should worry about whether they'd have an interest in me.

Goddess, how terrible would it be if those professors all had girlfriends...

Sorry About Your Parents

Delores

"Delores Drew! Where on earth have you been?" Lucille barks from the drawing room.

I'm not late; hell, I'm almost early.

Bruiser showed up at Shifter Secondary before the last bell rang, and I skipped out of my scintillating hemline conversation with the Heathers in plenty of time to get to the Escalade quickly. He drove straight home, and even with traffic, it took exactly the same time it always did.

Lucille simply has no idea what the hell time it is because it was martini o'clock hours ago, and she has difficulty staying lucid past four p.m. if the staff doesn't force her to eat. By staff, I mean Matilda, and when I cross the foyer to the drawing room to present myself, she gives me a small shake of her head. That means my dearest mother has consumed nothing but liquor all day and she likely hasn't left the house. It's Tuesday, so Julio the tennis pro must have canceled on her.

Given the day I've had, I don't have it in me to extend compassion to my inebriated maternal unit. Perhaps if she spent less time making me miserable and getting sloshed, she'd be pleasant enough for people who aren't getting paid to want her around.

Ouch.

The stress of today's tour and the random hot guy encounters have really put me in a weird mood.

I'm usually not quite this bitter, but...

"*Delores*! I can *smell* your fear, girl. Get in here!"

Rolling my eyes, I walk into the room, crossing to stand in front of her as she lounges on the couch in satin pajamas. She's definitely in a mood because her spotted tail is swishing near the floor, and her features are feline, but she's not fully shifted.

This does *not* bode well.

"I'm here, Lucille. What can I do for you?"

She snorts, tossing back her large martini as if it's water. "What can you do? What *can* you *do*? Hmmmm…"

Oh, no. Sharp and sarcastic Lucille is the worst one of them all.

My eyes dart towards the ceiling, then over to Matilda, and I catch another minuscule shake of her head. Bruno's not home, so I can't use him to distract my vodka soaked matriarch. This might be a bloodbath, and I know I did nothing wrong this time.

Truth be told, I never do, but that's never stopped either of my parents before, and it certainly won't now.

Lucille holds her glass out silently and I rush over to the pitcher, almost colliding with my former nanny in our haste to get the glass refilled before the leopard comes out for real. She rarely makes me feel like prey when she gets like this, but I'm fairly certain her personal version of the most dangerous game is why Matilda's eye twitches.

I walk over to my mother and pour her another round, sitting the crystal pitcher on the closest table so it stays within reach. "Yes,

Lucille. What can I do? Did I not get an excellent report from my visit to Apex today? Is that why you seem perturbed?"

That's my gentle way of asking if that's why she blasted at four p.m., though I doubt Lucille comprehends it.

"Your *visit* must have gone very well because I have not received a call telling me you need to be sent to Bloodstone. *However*, you *know* how I feel about tardiness, Delores!"

Tilting my head, I give her my best cowed expression. "I'm glad I could represent the family in a manner befitting the Drew name."

Her snort nearly knocks the glass out of her hand and she sloshes it towards me as she snarls, "No one would *ever* accuse you of that, Delores. You simply managed to not make a fool of us in public. A *prey* animal could do that."

I'm edging dangerously close to telling her to go fuck herself. *Danger, Delores Drew.* It's time to high-tail it out of here before this goes from bad to worse. What can I say to distract her? How can I get her to focus on something besides making me feel like crap?

"Lucille? I was wondering if Matilda would be available to take me dress shopping tomorrow? The prom is on Friday, and you haven't found time in your busy work schedule to go. I don't want to embarrass you further by showing up at the social event of the year dressed inappropriately. The Heathers all selected their gowns weeks ago, and I'm afraid I won't find something you approve of."

Her eyes narrow as she looks at me. "You want *her* to take you?"

Matilda looks terrified at the tone of Lucille's voice and I shake my head, keeping my voice even and calm. "Of course not, Lucille. You've got such a busy schedule, and I thought I would be less of a burden if Matilda escorted me."

"It would honor me to assist you and Delores, Madame, if you wish for me to do so."

Lucille lets out a heavy sigh, rolling her eyes as she waves her hand. "Fine, fine. Take her to Preyda, Dingo & Anaconda, and Yves St. Leopard. Avoid the others—their stylists have angered me this month."

Breathing a sigh of relief, I nod. "Understood. We'll go to the boutiques you recommend and I'll charge your house account. Thank you, Lucille. I'm very excited about my last dance at Shifter Secondary. I know it will be a night I'll remember for the rest of my life."

"Yes, yes. Teenage romance with that dimwit you call a boyfriend." She sips her martini again, giving me a calculating stare. "Prom should be a night to remember, I'm told. I'm happy to help you make that dream come true, Delores."

I pause, trying to decide if I should ask her what she means by that, but she waves me off as if I'm a fly buzzing around her.

Dipping my head, I mutter something about seeing her at dinner and make a break for it while she's waving her glass at Matilda for a refill.

Lucille always gets the last word in. I just don't know what those words meant this time.

⊖

ONCE I'VE ESCAPED TO THE RELATIVE SAFETY OF MY ROOM, I DROP my purse on my desk and breathe a sigh of relief. Clothes go flying as I peel off the stupid uniform, looking at myself in the mirror, observing my reflection thoughtfully.

I'm not bad looking, even if I'm not 'enhanced' like the Heathers. Lucille would probably jizz herself if I asked for any cosmetic procedures, but I don't think I need them. I'm not rail thin, but I'm thin enough to pull off crop tops and bikinis. I have a little 'junk in my trunk', which is what the Heathers just *love* to comment on. Between them and Todd's friends, they have lots of creative names for my curves, and it's annoying as hell.

The two boinking professors today seemed interested enough.

However, they're obviously *men*, not boys. Maybe when boys grow up, they stop acting like girls with meat on their bones are defective? *Hell if I know.* I just know that they let me watch them, and then the sexy blond got all up close and personal in the art room. Close enough to feel the girls and not be a jackass about my curves like everyone else is, which seems to show that I'm not a lost cause.

I wonder what they would have done if I'd continued my exploration earlier? My hormones have been out of whack since my eighteenth birthday, and if I'm honest, I spend more time helping myself than wanting to rub all over Todd. It's so odd, yet it doesn't feel wrong. Getting hot and heavy with *him* feels weird, and I've *never* felt the way I did during my encounters at Apex.

Do I have a fetish I don't know about? How does one even know that stuff?

It's not like I can Google it; my parents have spy software connected to our home network, and it invades every device within the walls. They had it on my phone, but Gold got the nerd from her dad's company to alter it so I can at least text and call in private. She promised to go on a date with him in return, but I think we all know that never happened. It gave me the freedom to communicate with my friends and boyfriends without the Osbournes downstairs listening in.

Speaking of which…

Grabbing my silk tank and short PJs, I shimmy them on and head for my bed. I pick up my phone and roll onto my back, holding it up as I click on the group chat with the Heathers. They'll be excited that I finally get to go pick out my dress, I'm sure.

DD: The royal bitch is letting Mattie take me to get my dress tomorrow!

SmackbookPrincess: It's about time. We were worried you'd have to Cinderella it.

FaithfulHeir: I've had mine since Christmas. Papi took us to Paris on a mission trip, and I bought it right off the runway.

DD: What kind of mission trip goes to Paris for Christmas?

FaithfulHeir: Zeus works in mysterious ways, DD. It's not ours to question where we are called.

BeanQueen: Stop it, H. You know your Mami just wanted to snub the British royals.

DuchessofDirt: C. is right, H. I had a stringer who has a crush on me. Check your story. Your dear old Papi is just as crooked as the rest of our parents. Own it.

Just like that, we're no longer talking about the topic I started. Pink's family—the Barringtons—control the largest news media conglomerate in the world. She uses information like cash, and although all she wants to do is spread 'fake news' about everyone, she won't hesitate to use her resources to out anyone she feels has wronged her.

We won't discuss what happened to that poor freshman who dared to wear the same Leopardtins as her last year. The puma shifter seemed to fade into nothingness after Pink launched her terror campaign on every social media and print channel she could access. I'm pretty sure she moved to a cave in the mountains of China—that's how scarce she was afterward.

Pink is straight up savage, and she'll turn on you in a hot second if she thinks it will benefit her.

DD: Where did the rest of you get your dresses? Sounds like H has a Clawnel.

SmackbookPrincess: Daddy had mine made by Vera Fang. It's one of a kind.

BeanQueen: Mine is from next spring's Grrsace collection—no one else has even seen it.

DuchessofDirt: I have an Alexangrr McQueen. He made the Princess' wedding gown, you know.

Sigh. Of course I know.

Their obsession with celebrities and royal families around the globe has always felt superficial. I can't believe how many hours they spent re-watching the most recent royal weddings and critiquing the clothing. They spend more time tearing into the clothing habits of famous people than they do on their school-work. I'm pretty sure their fathers all had to make a hefty dona-tion to get them admitted to Apex Academy with their poor grades.

It disappointed Bruno that he didn't need to bribe anyone—that's how I know.

DD: Mattie and I are going in the morning. Should I send pics while I try things on?

DuchessofDirt: Of course!

FaithfulHeir: We have to critique the dresses.

BeanQueen: Every. Single. One. DD.

SmackbookPrincess: We can't have you showing up looking like you don't belong. It's your big night.

I frown. Why are they so obsessed with talking about Todd and me having sex on prom night? Letting my animal emerge is a big deal in our society, but my friends are acting creepy as hell. I don't get it.

> DD: Well, I need to get downstairs for dinner before Lucille screams. Talk later?

> BeanQueen: Yep!

> SmackbookPrincess: Call me!

> DuchessofDirt: Don't let them make you grovel!

> FaithfulHeir: Don't be dramatic, DD. Text us later.

Sitting my phone on my bed, I rub my hands over my face. I don't know what I'd do without my friends, but sometimes, they are a bit much.

Lately...it's felt that way all the time.

The Bitch Is Back

Lucille

"You heard what I said, Henrietta. Call your counterpart at that useless school and explain the situation. I expect you to follow my instructions to the letter or there will be consequences."

The headmistress at Apex is a bald eagle shifter, and I've considered simply eating the stupid featherhead at least a dozen times over the years. The Council controls all schools—worldwide—and we strive to place teachers who will encourage our philosophy of ruthless domination over the prey animals.

However, we typically have to choose smaller predators as our administration puppets to prevent any uprising in the academic community. We specifically choose outcasts, ancient retirees, and those we can keep under our thumb via various blackmail schemes as the staff and professors at the various schools. The administration answers to the Council, but the Council answers to the Society.

As the Rostoff family representative in the Society, I know the last thing we need is some bleeding heart young pred convincing our heirs to sympathize with the plight of the downtrodden cousins.

Pathetic. I can't fathom anyone empathizing with the weaker species, but revolutions have started with less.

My family taught me loose ends always unravel, so I don't give them the chance to form. Bruno is less concerned with the bigger picture; he leaves that to me. His strength is in brute force and dealing with the bloodier side of my reign as the head of the Society. I maintain the more delicate relationships with the member families, negotiate the deals that fund our efforts, and help keep the darker side of our roster in the shadows.

The Khan empire and my father's operation in Europe and Asia remain feared, but their illegal activities stay concealed under my watch. They launder all the money that comes from their death matches, blackmail, trafficking, gambling, and theft through dozens of layers of shell corporations before it reaches the Society's coffers.

It's not the life I dreamed of as a girl, but it's better than ending up on the auction block as a child like my less cooperative sisters. Dmitri Rostoff is not a forgiving man, and I molded myself in his image to escape that fate.

Delores would do well to learn by my example and follow her parents' command, but she prefers to defy me at every turn. Bruno's threat about Bloodstone is far more generous than what my father offered my sisters. She should be grateful that death is an option.

When that birdbrain finally takes a breath, I growl into the phone. "Make it happen, Henrietta. I don't know what my rebellious spawn is planning for that night, but she will learn that she doesn't get to cross Lucille Natalia Rostoff. This is Delores' come to Zeus moment, and I'm eager to see her face when she finds out that I've ruined her perfect little night."

I look at my glass, scowling as I realize that it's empty. *"Matilda! Where are you, you useless tweety bird?"*

The twitchy shifter comes barreling in, her thick glasses askew and wisps of hair flying out of the tight bun she's required to wear. I swear, if Delores hadn't pointed out that hiring a more suitably attractive assistant might draw attention from my own sumptuous appearance, I would have sent the hawk packing once my spawn reached an age where she could reliably feed herself.

"My glass is empty."

Her eyes widen—appropriate since that's one of my finite rules—and she nearly trips on the endangered snow fox carpet as she hurries to rectify her idiocy.

Once I can sip the ice cold vodka again, I watch as my useless servant positions herself at the ready near the fireplace. I suspect Delores' bumbling behavior and incapability of merely following orders has to come from their long-term relationship, but I can't prove it. Matilda's as spineless as preds come, and no matter how hard I step on my progeny's neck to teach her obedience, her ex-nanny never opens her beak to complain.

Perhaps my daughter needs a firmer hand to make her realize she will *never* eclipse me—not in beauty, not in power, nor in the Society.

My daughter is going to bend her knee, or the consequences will be dire.

That, I can guarantee.

Little Black Dress

Delores

"Mattie! Bruiser brought the car around. Come on!"

I tap my foot anxiously, knowing that Lucille is probably purposely holding Matilda up to spite me. My mother has no interest in going dress shopping—she simply wants to make certain I don't acquire something befitting our 'standing' so she can say that I've disappointed the family again. Neither of my parents talk about their childhoods, but I can only imagine the type of family atmosphere that produced the parents who had so little interest in raising me.

The small, thin hawk shifter hurries out of the house, her large bag clutched to her side as she follows me toward the enormous Hummer. She waits for me to get in the back before sliding in next to me and shutting the door. I can feel the nervous energy radiating off of her as she watches the glaring Komodo in the front seat. Her fingers reach up to adjust her glasses and she clears her throat.

"Madame Lucille instructed me to have you visit Dingo & Anaconda first. She would like St. Leopard to be second, and

Preyda after that." Bruiser grunts and starts the car, and my ex-nanny turns to me. "She also added that if we do not find attire at those, we may visit Growlvinchy. All stores will have a dedicated attendant for us and shoe concierges. They will provide any other necessities the day of—I assume your father will open the vault to bring the needed jewels home."

Bringing my hands to my face, I hold back a scream. Now I know why he's been scarce. Bruno is running around gathering the ingredients for a press gaggle to be present at the prom on Friday. He'll force me to wear the family jewels for all to see, and that will cement me as the 'heir apparent all grown up' in the press.

I guess he got the idea of running around being a gross old man at the casinos with Pink's disgusting dad. The Barrington shark is a slimy, shifty eyed asshole, which is why I've never once agreed to spend the night at her house. Her 'Daddy' shit creeps me out.

"Mattie," I say, choosing my words carefully with Bruno's lackey in the driver's seat. "I'm very grateful that Lucille arranged all of this for me. Please let her know her personal attention was invaluable."

A tiny smile quirks at the corners of her mouth. Matilda has had years to interpret my appreciation for *her* efforts from compliments aimed at my mother. No one can ever outshine Lucille, and despite her complete lack of interest in anything but berating me, she cannot bear for me to treat Mattie kindly. I don't know if it's pride or some small part of her that recognizes what a pitiful excuse for a parent she is. Either way, I've always made sure that Mattie gets the thanks she richly deserves.

The car falls silent for the duration of the trip into the city, and the time passes quickly. I text the Heathers to let them know what our game plan is, and of course, they all have their own suggestions for what area of the stores I should start with. I'm not as familiar with the designers as they are—I order my clothes online, and I don't favor high-end fashion houses. I'd much rather wear clothes that are comfortable than things that feel like a costume.

The car stops abruptly in front of a store and Bruiser turns around. "We're here. Get your things. I won't wait."

Matilda blinks behind her thick round frames, and I give her a reassuring pat on her hand. Bruiser will not throw us out the door and take off, but he won't waste time, either. She doesn't know how he behaves without my parents around, so I know it must be making her nervous. "Thank you, Bruiser. We will have the final store contact you when we are ready to be picked up."

His rough grunt is the only response and Matilda looks at me with wide eyes. I smile again, waiting for the car to slow to stop in front of the house of Dingo & Anaconda. Generations ago, this unlikely pairing of preds created a design alliance, and their collections have been coveted by the rich and famous.

I'm uncertain they will have anything I would be caught dead wearing, but Lucille insisted. Last spring, they featured a bunch of weird mismatched, patchwork designs that looked like Franken-clothes. Lucille bought several pieces with bold black and white checkerboard patterns that made her look like she was trying to relive the 70s, and I couldn't even look at her without having to smother a giggle.

As we enter the boutique, I feel the change in the air. I wouldn't put it past the high-end fashion houses to pump in pred-stasy through the filtration system to encourage large purchases. Although it's shady, the drug is as legal as caffeine, and you'd have to prove they dosed their customers.

Good luck with that... most shoppers are already drunk or on some form of upper when they arrive, anyway. None of my friends' parents would submit to a drug test voluntarily, and mine would probably eat the unfortunate soul who had to ask.

"It's very..." Matilda whispers.

I sigh and nod my head, appreciating that she already knows nothing here is my style. "It is. But we'll start here and work our way through Lucille's suggestions. Maybe I'll find something not awful in one of them. It is pretty close to the wire, though, and most of the designers have probably signed exclusivity contracts with the elite families."

"Welcome to Dingo & Anaconda," the smarmy looking concierge gushes. "Your mother has called ahead to have us put aside a selection of gowns in your size. Follow me to the dressing lounge. Would you like champagne? Maybe something stronger?"

Giving him a wide berth, I shake my head. Mattie looks like she could use a scotch, but I will not get either of us busted for imbibing by accepting anything this creep offers. "No, thank you. May I ask what size Luc—my mother told you? I want to make sure we have it correct to reduce the amount of oils from hands on your lovely designs."

"But of course! Your mother asked us to pull dresses in a size four and six."

"Delores will need you to re-stock those and find the same designs in a size twelve. I'm afraid mothers never want their daughters to grow up," Mattie interjects before I lose my temper in front of the slimy little toad.

I should have known.

Lucille purposefully told the designers I am several sizes smaller than I am to humiliate me. I'm going to have this conversation at every store we visit today if I don't find a dress that suits me here. Her cruelty knows no bounds—truly. She's determined to make me feel like shit. I can only assume this is her revenge for asking if Matilda could take me.

I enter the dressing room and wait for Mr. Creepy Weasel to bring the pre-approved dresses back in the right size. When he knocks on the door, I open it and my chest caves. They are all big, fluffy princess gowns... I'd be right at home in Disney World with all the cartoon characters roaming around. I don't want to dress like I'm going to ride in a pumpkin carriage.

Damn Lucille. She'd never wear something this ridiculous, and she knows I wouldn't want to, either. That leopard thinks of everything and I'm going to have to work hard to escape her clutches some day.

With a heavy sigh of frustration, I try on the marshmallow gowns, snapping pics for the Heathers as I go. At least I'll have evidence that I gave Lucille's suggestions a fair try.

"Delores, if you don't find a dress at Growlvinchy, your mother will be furious!" Matilda frets, looking around us as we walk down the ritzy boulevard. "She insisted we choose a piece from the designers she is currently pleased with."

"I know, Mattie, but she had every store pull every stupid poofy meringue dress they had in their stockroom. It was her idea of a joke, and every one of the personal shoppers at the stores we were in refused to show me anything else. I can *not* go to my prom dressed like Cinderella!"

The hawk shifter sighs, straightening her glasses as we approach the sleek obsidian marble of the Growlvinchy boutique. This designer was *not* on her list last night, and I'd love to know what underhanded deal Lucille worked out to get me in here. It has to be substantial because we know Gautier Growlvinchy likes to give the finger to anyone he doesn't like, even those as powerful as Lucille.

A pangolin valet opens the double doors of the elite showroom and we step inside. They perfumed the air with a customized scent and I inhale, trying to catch the notes. The small, obsequious animal bows to us, his claw-like hands clasped together as he does so.

"You're smelling violet, musk, freesia, sandalwood, and a few other top secret ingredients. Can't give away the farm, I'm afraid, but I'll give you a hint."

My eyes widen as I realize the impeccably dressed predator who just joined us is Gautier himself. His legendary wild mane of striped hair falls to his shoulders, just barely touching the shiny black sharkskin suit. His bow tie, pocket square, and shoes are a fiery orange with matching stripes—the world-famous signature of the best dressed tiger in pred-dom.

"I…"

"Tut, tut, Miss Drew. It's unbecoming for a young lady of your stature to babble. Follow me to the VIP lounge. I will begin with a fitting, regardless of what I was asked prior to you arriving, before I choose the designs. I find it makes for a more satisfying experience for everyone involved."

For a moment, both shock and gratitude war within me, and Matilda reaches over to shut my mouth gently. No one defies Lucille—her wrath has destroyed entire industries—but this incredibly odd fashion diva seems wholly unconcerned whether his executive decisions will get back to her.

Swallowing hard, I whisper, "Thank you. I can't express how much I appreciate your approach, Monsieur Growlvinchy."

His sharp bark of laughter fills the gilded room, and he shakes his head. "Oh, no, Miss Drew. If you are to wear my creations, we will become friends. My friends call me Luc. And you are?"

"Delores," I murmur.

"That simply will not do! A luscious predator like you cannot be called something so… pedestrian. I will ponder on it as we begin." He claps his large hands and a virtual fleet of pangolins comes waddling out to usher us towards the back of the store. They are making a weird chuffing sound as they scurry alongside us.

"Luc, are these your assistants? I've never seen designers allow prey animals to shift fully in front of them without threatening to eat them all the time." Growlvinchy's control is impressive.

"That's a fabulous question! Usually clients simply ignore my friends here as if they are furniture. This is an entire colony that I've gathered from unsafe situations during my travels. Emile is their leader—you met him at the door—and although they are usually solitary prey animals, they all live in a group in my compound."

Tilting my head, I give the tiger a confused look. "That seems like a very... unusual living arrangement for a predator." He laughs again, his golden eyes dancing as he opens the door to another room.

He walks me over to a raised area in the center of the lavish lounge, holding his hand out to help me step up onto the platform. "It is. However, I have lived long enough and traveled widely enough to know that the status quo is boring and often allows for tyranny. I have enough fortune and fame to allow me leeway to do things that make me happy, and having my friends safe and happy is one of those things. Plus, after I met Emile on an Asian tour, I learned that his kind have absolutely astounding talents for fabric and fine detail work, which of course makes them perfect allies for me."

I ponder that as Matilda takes a seat on the plush chaise, crossing her ankles as she watches me. Luc buzzes around me as he takes my measurements, occasionally asking me to move a limb or turn as he shouts the numbers to the pangolin, taking notes on a thick notepad. From toes to my nose, he checks every single curve and line to make sure he has it written.

When he finishes with the measuring tape, he sighs and smiles at me. "Ah, the Botticelli-esque lines of unenhanced figures. I rarely see it anymore. Okay, delightful girl. Hop over to your minder and tell me what kind of dress you wish you could own."

This is not the experience I expected when we walked through the doors of one of the most famous designers in the world, but it's definitely the best thing we've done all day. I sit next to Matilda, thinking for a moment before I respond. "Something that doesn't make me feel like a child playing dress up."

"*Oui! Parfait!*" he exclaims, turning on his heel and heading for the back room. "I shall return with your dress."

Turning to Matilda, I whisper, "This is weird, right? I mean, I'm supposed to try things on. Gold liked that Preyda, and Purple thought the pink St. Leopard looked good. Should I have gotten those? Luc is so nice, but how can he know what I need from... that?"

"Delores, I don't think the dresses they gave you were right for you. Your friends... may have been trying to... look on the bright side. Make something good out of your mother's suggestions. So they picked what they felt was the least objectionable option."

Even my ex-nanny doesn't look convinced by her own words, but if she wanted to say more, she would. I nod, chewing my lip as I worry. "If we don't find the right thing here, Lucille will win. Again. It will ruin the biggest night of my life."

"Oh, my," the hawk shifter whispers.

I expected Matilda to accept my choice to take the next step with Todd. I thought she liked him—at least a little—and I frown, ready to open my mouth to defend him. Instead, I feel her hand gently grab my chin and turn my face towards the other side of the room.

Luc walks in with a single black dress held aloft on its hanger. The satin shimmers in the low light, accentuating the mermaid cut and long train the pangolin is holding off the floor as they follow him. It looks like modern design meets Holly Golightly, and it's amazing. I think I saw T. Swift wear something like it at the Grammys one year.

"The sweetheart neckline paired with off-the-shoulder straps will accentuate your curves and long neck. If I'm right—and I always am—the hourglass shape will highlight every curve, and the train will force you to walk with an elegant gait. Too many women rush their entrance… it's the anticipation that makes the presentation striking," Growlvinchy says, his expression amused.

Another pangolin rushes forward, its claws dangling a pair of four-inch heels in black satin with very thin straps at the ankles and toes. They covered the straps and heels in sparkling diamonds, and if they're real, this will put a dent in Lucille's fun money account like no other. They don't have the telltale red sole of Leopardtins when I peek underneath. That's odd—those are the hottest shoes in the world at the moment.

Luc claps his hands again, looking delighted. "Good eye, delightful girl! I did not pick shoes from my great friend Leopartin for you because *all* the girls will wear them. These are handmade by my colleague and occasional date, Messier Stuart Pyzman. They are the *crème de la crème* of exclusivity. He only fashions less than a hundred pairs of shoes a year."

"Are you sure I should wear shoes that are so…delicate?" I ask, almost afraid to touch something so beautiful and expensive.

"You should try it on, Delores," Matilda says softly, giving me a small smile. "I believe Monsieur Growlvinchy has outdone himself."

Blinking, I rise to my feet, bolstered by the encouragement of those around me. If they think I'm worthy of such lovely designs… then maybe I am?

The pangolin holding the shoes crooks a claw at me and I nod, following the creature as it waddles towards an area with a curtain for me to change behind. Stepping into the tiny room, I wait for the tiger to hang the garment on the rack and close my eyes.

Lucille will be furious with me for choosing something so unlike what she selected. But maybe it's time for me to do what the Heathers suggested and grow a pair of fangs.

After all, prom will be the first night of my life as a true predator, and after that, my parents won't be able to control me anymore.

It's time to grow up, Delores Diamond Drew.

I Feel Like I'm Drowning

Felix

Today's classes were an absolute shitshow. Springtime is the worst time of year to be a professor in this place because once the ruts and heat cycles begin, the spoiled idiots here are a lost cause. At least, the underclassmen are, and that's what I'm stuck teaching.

Many upperclassmen do their exchange semesters during this season, so the poor schmucks at our sister schools end up dealing with their lack of control. But here? The rich, pampered kids who have barely emerged start feeling things we haven't properly instructed them on and it's a goddamn nightmare. My childhood was no picnic, but at least my asshole father had people teach me how my fucking body worked after the emergence ceremony.

The ceremony is a whole different story, since it's why I'm here teaching these numbskulls instead of ruling my ambush as I should be.

"Feeeeeelix," a low sultry voice calling for me as I stomp across campus to the staff village where my miniature ambush lives. "Are you coming out tonight, baby?"

I don't stop. The owner of that voice is not someone I want to be around, given my mood. She's obviously hoping for a repeat of our occasional mutual frustration relief and it's not going to happen. I'm sure she'll be decked out in some skimpy designer nonsense designed to barely cover her curves if I turn around. She's extremely attractive, and she knows it; however, my poor judgment in bedding her in the past resulted in this behavior. I don't feel self-destructive enough to encourage this today.

"Get lost, Zhenga," I snarl over my shoulder.

Maybe that will deter her, but it's doubtful.

Zhenga Leonidas is the eldest daughter of the famed Leonidas pride. Behavior like this is exactly why her mother had her sent to Apex and outside of trying to land one of the bigger fish in the staff pond, she's never even tried to wriggle out of her sentence here. I think unless she finds a catch to claim her, she's content to stay out of her family's reach and live it up on the weekends.

"Aw, baby, don't be like that! A bunch of us are going to party in town and we'd *love* for you to join us, Felix. You have the best *moves* of anyone here," she coos as she catches up with me.

Snorting at her lack of subtlety, I feel my cock practically jump back inside of my body. There are plenty of connected shifters working at Apex—cast out kings, alphas, betas, rajs, rexes—I'm not the only one she's taken a ride on. I don't give a flying fuck how promiscuous she is, but I care that she's an opportunist seeking to land a powerful husband to please her mother. That kind of desperation eventually leads to poking holes in condoms and faking birth control. Cubs are something I'm not remotely interested in and I sure as hell don't want them with her.

Plus, our families pushed Zhenga and her sisters at Fitz and me from the time we were young.

The Leonidas pride is the second largest clan of cat shifters in the world, and they own majority stakes in every major sports league for preds. They're not as feared or powerful as the Khans, though.

Marrying one of us would merge our wealth and influence enough to alter the balance of the Council forever. Unfortunately for the Leonidas lioness, her daughters grew too comfortable living the famous socialite life and anyone with half a brain refused to let their heirs tie themselves to them. Zhenga's older sister went completely off-the-rails while they were partying in Ibiza and crashed in a tunnel a few years before my exile. She died on impact and Z got sent here until she learned her lesson.

By the time they banished me from my home, she'd settled into this place like the reigning queen of the staff. You'd think my status would discourage her, but it seems to make her even more determined to land me. I made the mistake of getting with her in a few *very* drunken hook-ups when I first arrived, and I've been paying for it ever since. Nobody was shocked because I made a poor decision that resulted in me being sent here. Both Fitz and Chess threaten to punch me in balls every time she speaks to me in front of them, but that's because Chess is usually stuck prying her off of me.

I'm such a fucking asshole I can't even clean up my own messes.

"Zhenga, I've told you a thousand times and I'll keep saying it until you get it through your thick skull." I come to a stop at the entrance to the staff housing, whirling around to look at her with the full force of the Raj in my eyes. "I do not want a repeat performance of the idiotic choices I made when I was soaked in booze twenty-four hours a day when I arrived at this hellhole. Not here on campus, and *definitely* not at some sticky floored, techno blasting college club where staff pretend we aren't geriatric compared to the intended patrons."

Letting out an angry rumble, the lioness stalks closer to me, getting in my face as she glares. That she can hold my gaze for even a small amount of time when I'm pushing my Raj influence onto her confirms she *should* be the heir to the Leonidas pride rather than her spineless cousin. But even the amount of power that gives her eventually falters as I continue to press her. When she finally ducks her head, I give her a grin full of fangs before turning my back on her to walk away.

"Lie to yourself all you want, Felix, but you'll be back. Even if you won't give me your giant cock again, you need someone who will fight you without reservation in the ring. You can't get rid of me that easily, you coward!"

I grit my teeth as I storm across my yard and slam into the house. *She's not wrong and I hate myself for it.* It takes a moment for me to calm down long enough to realize Fitz is here and when I do; I thank the fucking stars for it. He's not as good at calming me as Chess is, but few people are as good at soothing beasts as my twin's consort.

However, the scent of my twin and the devotion he has to our small ambush always makes my tiger preen with approval. For a shifter born to rule, it's difficult to be shoved into a situation without a clan of their people to care for—in fact, if Fitz and Chess hadn't left with me, I might not have survived the first few months here.

Those two are my *actual* family and always will be. As much as I'd like to return home triumphantly so I can take back my rightful title and execute the traitorous assholes who suggested he banish me, I realize it wouldn't fix me. The betrayal of my consort, my parents, and the few younger siblings who hadn't died in the ambush trials before we left won't heal until I'm ready to forgive myself. I chose my happiness over that of my people and have been disgusted with myself ever since.

That's how I ended up staying so sauced I fucked Zhenga a couple of times in the first few months we lived here, by the way.

"Did thirsty Z catch you on the way in, bro?" Fitz gives me an amused look as he bumps my shoulder until I follow him to the couch.

Once I join him, he rubs his cheek on mine, then lays his head on my shoulder like he has since we were kids. He knows I need it—

after my disastrous affair with the lioness, I've denied myself physical contact with anyone not in my little family or fighting me in the ring. It kills me, but Chess and Fitz do their best to help my tiger get what it needs, so I don't go on a fucking rampage.

Neither of them thinks I should be punishing myself for what happened, but I can't seem to let it go. The throne at Bloodstone will always drip with the blood of both the guilty and the innocent, but Fitz and I always planned to change some of the more barbaric bullshit our great-great-great-grandparents instituted.

We were waiting for me to inherit the crown so we could get rid of things like the ambush trials, the emergence ceremony, and the punishment hunts. Those things impacted all three of us as cubs, including Chess, and we wanted better for our people. Our tigers are bloodthirsty and occasionally cruel, but the generations before us devolved into savagery and it needs to change.

But it never will now that we're stuck here for the rest of our lives and that's why I deserve to suffer.

"Yes, she did." I rub my cheek on the top of his head, wanting to replace the scent of the lioness with my twin's spicy juniper berry and ginger smell that's laced with hints of vetiver and sandalwood I know is from Chess. "Did you defile Aubrey's library again, Fitzy?"

He grins against my shoulder, shrugging a little. "It's the most private place on campus."

Groaning, I flop my head back on the couch. "Unlike our fucking house? One of these times, I'm going to let that grumpy bastard crisp you simply because you *ask* for it."

"I don't beeeelieeeeve you," Fitz sing-songs. "But you need to have more fun, bro. Taunting Aubrey and fucking Chessie are my guilty pleasures, but you don't have the luxury of either. You can't rely on beating the snot out of Pred Games contenders and staff members forever. This Fall, you need to find a playmate who isn't a psycho stalker."

I snort, rolling my head back and forth. "Absolutely not, Fitz. Idiots like me are the crown jewels of cock in this place. We only draw the psychos because they want to use us as a ticket out."

"Maybe a different pond? Chess and I saw this hot little number in the courtyard today and she damn near made his dick explode on Aubrey's precious windows in the sci-fi section." Fitz bobs his brows, completely unashamed of their antics in public or lusting after an incoming student.

"Fitz, that dragon will stomp you into the mud if you don't quit messing with his lair. You *know* what happened to that wolf alpha the year after we got here. He dared to mess with the book system and Aubrey turned him into a pile of charcoal before mailing his ashes to his former pack with a dragon turd."

My brother throws his head back and howls with laughter. "Fuck, I forgot about that. It might have been the funniest shit I've ever seen—old, stodgy scaly pants was so proud of himself. Rightly so, to be honest, because I would have paid good money to see the look on that fucker's face when his prodigal son arrived as sooty dragon shit in a paper bag."

I arch a brow at him as if to say, 'that's what I'm trying to tell you'.

"Don't worry, Felix. Aubrey loves me and I gave him a little project that should keep him busy for a while. Knowing how much he loves to research things, I figure I've got a couple weeks before he notices Chess and I have been sneaking in again."

That makes my entire body go tense.

"You're my brother, so I'm going to ask as your family, not your Raj. Is this more bullshit you're looking into because you want to help me fight the exile? You know I've asked you nicely to stop it." He shrugs and gives me a wink that does not fill me with confidence. I rub a hand over my face, letting out a heavy sigh as I look at the ceiling. "Fitz, if anyone from Bloodstone finds out, you'll get all of us killed!"

"Meh, we'll be fine." Fitz rubs his cheek on me again, completely unconcerned with the thought of our entire ambush's wrath coming down on us. He's always been the perfect representation of everything my father wanted me to be—outside of his feelings for Chess. My twin is morally flexible, unflinching at the prospect of danger, and a total psycho in battle; he's a Khan, through and through. "The dipshit sitting in your chair wouldn't last two minutes in the ring with either of us, even if he is our kin."

He's not wrong about that, either.

"But we're here and this is our life now, Fitz. Nothing can undo some things."

His growl is soft, but full of meaning. "Every single person who sided with our father and brother, the bitch who broke you, and the rest of the family members who did nothing will suffer at my hands for stealing what is yours, Felix. If they thought I was crazy when I was headed for the Pred Games, they have no idea what I'm capable of when I'm playing for vengeance. Blood will fill the halls and stain the tiles of that palace when I'm through."

I want to revel in the sincerity of my twin, but I know better than to give myself even a moment of peace. I don't deserve it, and even the smallest amount of mercy might lead to more. We can't take on our entire family and all of their allies—I'm fully aware of that. Fitz just needs something to believe in because he doesn't let anyone but Chess and me in, despite being one of the most social people I know. We're all stuck in this place because of me and I can't take away the one thing he's holding onto.

"You didn't let me tell you about the girl."

I smile to myself. When Fitz pouts, he's calm. "She must be something pretty fucking special if Chess looked up from your crotch to notice her."

Fitz barks a laugh, looking up at me with sparkling eyes. "Fuck yeah, she was. Stacked like a brick house, curves you can hang onto, eyes like the summer sky, and long blond hair you wanna wrap around your fist like a leash. Chessie said he wants to *fuck* her; can you believe it?"

Holy fuck.

"He did? Are you okay with that?" I ask curiously. Fitz can be possessive, but since his consort has never shown an ounce of interest in anyone but my brother, I have no baseline for this.

"And she's *unemerged*," he breathes like it's a prayer.

"Fitz…" I warn, looking at him with a dark glare. "We both know how dangerous that is. Let her figure out how stupid it would be to come here without ditching that attribute on her own. Neither you nor Chess need to be within five hundred feet of an unemerged rich brat, no matter how fucking hot she is."

"Relax, bro. Neither of us laid a finger on her, but looking at her made me hard enough to cut the fucking window glass."

He winks, and I roll my eyes. That had to be fun for Chess to deal with. Luckily for him, shifters heal quickly and Fitz might be rough, but he treats his consort like he's the prince instead of us. "You didn't answer me."

"Ugh, Felix, you're like a dog with a bone instead of a tiger." He grumbles and socks my thigh before continuing. "I told Chess I'd fucking love to make kitty sandwiches with whatever animal that girl turns out to be. I couldn't get a bead on it in the library, but then my lovely pin-up girl showed up in the gym during my afternoon workout. She joined a group of bobbleheaded twits babbling about being DTF at college parties and I got too distracted to suss it out. I'd guess she's from one of the Council lines after seeing her friends."

DTF? What in the hell does… oh.

That makes me feel positively ancient and I glare at my trend hopping twin for making me feel every single one of my thirty-six years with one off-hand phrase. "So what? I'm sure they're hoping to snag a rich asshole for a mate before they even have to waste their time on studying next year."

"Stop thinking about that salty lioness. I feel you tensing up," Fitz says as he rumbles next to me. "My point was that this sweet treat didn't seem comfortable with their mouthy shit. She might hold out for something real, if you can believe it. She obviously didn't know her friends are emerged; they were lying to her."

I squint at him. *Does this actually bother him? Did playboy Fitz Khan's heart grow two sizes today?* Pursing my lips, I suppress a grin. "I feel you want more from this girl than a simple fuck fest."

Fitz snorts and shakes his head. "Never, bro. Chess is the only permanent figure in this dick's future, but I'll happily swizzle about when I get the chance."

We'll see about that, little brother. We'll see.

Don't Let Me Get Me

As Bruiser pulls the car around to the front of the house, I look over at Matilda. Her shoulders are tight again, and she keeps pushing her glasses up her nose. I know she's worried because we don't have a dress to show Lucille, but Luc insisted that he would finish a few tweaks tonight and have it messenger'd over with the shoes in the morning. I'm not sure if that was a feint to keep Lucille from shredding it ahead of time or if he truly wanted to do a few alterations based on his notes.

It's not an unfounded concern; Lucille will *definitely* blow a gasket when we get inside. Since I see Bruno's MG outside, I know that means he'll join in the fun as well. This is going to be terrible, and there's nothing I can do to stop it. I give Matilda an encouraging smile, hoping to convey without words that we're not about to face an actual firing squad.

At least, I don't think Lucille will have one waiting, but who the hell knows with her?

Climbing out of the Hummer, I walk up the stairs, straightening my shoulders and securing the mask I have to wear when I deal with my parents. Matilda follows me quietly, staying a few steps behind like Lucille prefers staff to do. I hate it, but I know she's doing it to give the illusion that I'm following the same protocols the other heirs do.

"*Delores!*"

The wail of my fully loaded maternal unit permeates the heavy front door, and I suck in a deep breath. That's not good *at all*. I open the door, stepping into the gaudy marble foyer and heading for the drawing room. "Coming, Lucille!"

When I enter the drawing room, my mother is draped over her favorite chaise and my father is prowling the room like he's looking for fresh meat. Lucille has her traditional vodka martini and Bruno is carrying a hefty pour of scotch in a highball. The look in their eyes says they've grown bored with throwing insults at one another and I've now presented the perfect target with my arrival.

"How disappointing! You didn't find a suitable gown. Whatever will you wear to your prom?" Lucille sneers, her eyes lighting with satisfaction.

"Typical," my father growls. "She can't even spend money properly. I don't know how we produced such a *useless* heir. It must be your genes, Lucille; none of the women in my family are so inept."

Lucille rolls to her feet with the grace of a feline shifter, her eyes narrowing to slits. Ignoring Bruno, she advances on me, the predator inside of her shimmering beneath her skin as she moves. "That*'s* what happened, isn't it? Speak up, Delores!"

Matilda scurries towards the bar cabinet as the vodka sloshes out of Lucille's glass, anticipating her next order. I mutely shake my head at my mother, swallowing as I decide how I'm going to explain my lack of a garment without setting her off. I'm never sure how to handle her when she's this sloshed, but with Bruno in the mix, I have even less confidence that I'll come out of this situation unscathed.

"Oh, I know what happened. You don't have to admit your shame out loud. Not one designer had anything left that fit your... *ample* frame." Lucille's eyes sparkle with delight as she continues to stalk towards me. "You should have allowed me to make that appointment with Dr. Randall. We could have nipped your baby fat in the bud long before this disaster."

My eyes widen and my hand flies to my mouth of its own volition. I strive to not give Lucille the reaction she craves, but after the sizing fiasco she engineered and now this, she's hit all the right notes to destroy what little confidence I have. "I... I... No. Um, Monsieur Growlvinchy… there are alterations."

"Madame," Matilda intervenes, handing Lucille a fresh drink while staying as far away from Bruno as possible. "The boutique will send Delores' dress tomorrow morning by messenger. A few small things needed to be tailored, but I did not wish Delores to be home late, so they will get completed overnight."

Bruno whirls, glaring at the hawk shifter. "Did she ask you? Know your place, featherhead."

I wince. I know Mattie was only trying to help, and my parents are just about as awful as they can be to her without being physically violent. Although that could change at any moment, I suppose. "I apologize, Father. I got a little tongue tied and I'm sure Matilda only wished to inform you of the special consideration Monsieur Growlvinchy afforded us. He was quite complimentary of Lucille, and he provided us with only the finest designs."

That's not a lie, but not exactly the truth, either. It seems to mollify Bruno for the moment. Lucille continues to glare at me, her suspicious nature keeping her from trusting anyone's word. I stand perfectly still—like prey—waiting for her to decide what to do next. She finally heads back to the lounge, dropping onto it with a sigh of irritation.

"He probably has to re-stitch every seam to fit you. Couture isn't suitable for your body."

Her words hit me like a brick between the eyes, and I turn on my heel, running for the stairs without waiting to be excused. I refuse to give her the satisfaction of seeing me cry, and if I didn't escape right now, that was going to happen.

My parents' drunken laughter echoes through the hallway as I choke back a sob.

Just another day at the Drew House of Horrors.

THE DOOR CLOSES BEHIND ME WITH A SLAM THAT RATTLES THE frame, and I dive for my bed, burying my face in my soft pillows. My mother has always known how to dig under my skin until I'm raw, and she never shies away from making me feel like the worst daughter she could have ever birthed. I don't know why I let her, but I can't help feeling abandoned when the two people who are supposed to love me unconditionally seem to loathe my existence.

I often wonder why they had me, but I know the answer to that question. The elite families have to produce an heir to keep in power, and if there's one thing my parents love more than booze, it's power. I'm not sure why they didn't have another child to replace me, since I'm such a disappointment, but I've pondered it many times over the years.

In similar situations, the next in line either kills the first born—depending on species—or the parents disown the eldest child. If mine disowned me, I'd be penniless, but I'd be free, and I'm sure I could figure out how to survive. But Lucille and Bruno chose violence instead of replacing me—they've simply spent my entire life beating me down so they can marry me off, increase our family's power and social standing and use my husband as their proxy.

There's no way Todd will let them treat me this way once we're married. He may have his moments, but he's good and kind, and he loves me. I'm sure we're mates, even if I haven't felt all of that stuff the internet says I should. I assume it's because we haven't taken the last step yet, but that will change on prom night. Once our animals emerge, we'll recognize one another as soulmates.

Right?

When the tears finally stop flowing, I tear off my clothes, tossing them in the hamper and putting on my comfy pajamas. I refuse to go down for dinner, but if I'm lucky, Matilda will sneak something upstairs. My phone buzzes from my handbag, and I sigh.

It has to be the Heathers. The last time I texted was before I found the dress at Growlvinchy's and I didn't send them a photo of that one. But these girls are like sharks swimming around an injured fish with gossip, and I'm surprised I got away with it for this long.

SmackbookPrincess: DD! Where the hell are you???!!!

BeanQueen: Not cool, DD. We showed you our dress.

FaithfulHeir: Did you strike out? What are you gonna do?

DuchessofDirt: I'll bet she struck out. That's why she's not answering. She'll have to buy off the rack. Scandalous, DD.

SmackbookPrincess: DD, you can't buy off the rack! We're all riding in the limo Todd rented, and we cannot show up with someone dressed like a peasant.

DuchessofDirt: Daddy would be fit to be tied. It would be all over Fangbook and Instagrowl in a matter of minutes.

I sigh. The only reason it would end up on social media would be because *she* would post it, but that's an argument I'm not emotionally prepared to have this evening. Even if they are kind of the worst, I could really use my friends tonight. They won't sugarcoat anything, but they will distract me from Lucille's hurtful words echoing in my head.

> DD: Guys? I found a dress, but it's not here. It needed some tiny tweaks, and Lucille lost the plot. Can you guys sneak in for girls' time? It would make me feel a lot better.

> SmackbookPrincess: Oh, hell yeah! I mean, it sucks you can't fit into things, DD, but we'll come and bring some refreshments to drown your sorrows in.

> FaithfulHeir: We're on our way once we get a ride. Have the window open.

> BeanQueen: I've got snacks.

> DuchessofDirt: We'll get the full scoop when we get there, DD. See you soon!

Tossing my phone on the bed, I walk over to my keyboard and sit down. We could absolutely afford a gorgeous baby grand for me to compose on, but Lucille hates my 'time wasting drivel'. She's never supported my songwriting or my love of music, and this was the closest thing I could weasel out of my parents. It cost me quite a few awful dinner functions and a couple of society ball appearances, but it's my only outlet, and I love it.

My fingers brush over the keys, stretching as I warm up. The girls won't leave their houses for at least an hour—since they'll be primping, even for a sleepover—and it will take another thirty minutes to get here. I've got time to work out some of this heartache.

'... and I look in the mirror again, but I don't see what you see...'

The chords flow as I work on the lyrics to a tune that no one will ever hear as I sing along, my voice low and husky. I'm not an alto, not really, but I have to sing quietly so they won't hear me and show up to ruin my escape.

My real range falls into mezzo soprano—or I think it does based on the tutorials I've done on YouTube. Without real lessons, I can only follow along with voice teachers and Broadway stars in their videos and hope I'm not terrible. Lucille never let me take voice because it wasn't as socially *useful* as dance; I have to do what I can on my own.

I don't dare ask my friends or even Todd if I'm any good. It'd be too demoralizing to find out my one genuine passion is something I suck at. I chose English as my major at Apex so I can better craft my lyrics—despite the line of bull I fed Lucille about using my degree to further our family's standing through public appearances and speeches at charity functions.

'… if only your love could set me free…'

Sighing again, I look at the picture of Todd and me at Winter Formal, cheesing for the camera. Truer words have never been spoken, and it won't be long before the love between Todd and I sets my animal—and my future—free.

Only one more day…

Look At Me, I'm Sandra Dee

Delores

"We're heeeeere!"

The deafening cry from below my window makes me cringe. It's possible the Heathers pre-gamed on the way here—judging from the not stealthy screech—and I immediately regret my choice to invite them over. That volume may not rouse Lucille or Bruno from their nightly stupor, but that asshole Bruiser doesn't drink a drop and neither do the thick necks on his security team. If one of them hears, we're all busted.

"Shhh!" I hiss out the window, dumping the rope ladder out so it unfurls to the ground with a soft thump. "You know Bruiser prowls the grounds at night."

"Oh, he loooooves me," Silver giggles.

My eyes narrow and I squint down at her, trying to suss out what she means. Bruiser doesn't like anyone he's not torturing, but T is an odd duck even at the best of times. Her dad isn't a creepy 'daddy' like Pink's, but Silver has always given off a vibe that isn't quite right. However, I have too much to worry about without going down this rabbit hole.

"Whatever, guys. Just get up here before security finds you and we all have to stand in front of Lucille to explain why you're sneaking at this time of night."

The girls do their best to scramble up the ladder in their inebriated state, the clinking bags on their backs full of alcohol making it a much more harrowing experience than it needs to be. I suck in a breath, watching the ladder sway back and forth as each one ascends, and I don't let it out until the very last Heather is inside my room.

"Did you guys get blasted before you got here?" I ask, wrinkling my nose as Silver giggles in my face with enough gin on her breath to make me fail a breathalyzer.

"*Of course* we did. You're such a stick in the mud, DD. You never want to try *anything*," Gold grumbles from behind me.

I turn, my mouth dropping open as they ditch their trench coats to reveal ridiculously sexy lingerie rather than pajamas. What the fuck is this, the Victoria's Secret Pred Show? I mean, we're gonna lie around my room and bitch about our parents, not perform at the Moulin Rouge. "What the hell are you all wearing?"

In true Heather fashion, they've donned matching teddies with garters, thigh highs, and heels, only varying in color. Their hairstyle of the day is high ponytails, and they're made up within an inch of peeling their faces off with a palette knife. Conversely, I look like a dead fish in the water wearing my plain PJs and no makeup, which doesn't help me feel better about Lucille's earlier comments.

"We figured we could give you a *makeover*!" Pink exclaims, grabbing her backpack from the floor. She unzips it, dumping it on the bed to reveal a mini-fridge worth of airplane bottles of booze and a shit ton of makeup.

Silver gives me a smirk that makes my ass twitch as she does the same, bottles and products clinking as they join Pink's on the comforter. I watch as Purple and Gold do the same, though a suspicious bag of white pills is the last thing to escape Gold's bag. My eyes narrow as I look at them all, salivating at the prospect of turning me into one of them.

Something isn't right here, and I don't know what.

It feels weird, but that's probably just leftover nerves from dealing with my scheming maternal unit. These guys may be shallow and bitchy, but they're my best friends and would never do anything to truly hurt me.

"I don't know, guys. I mean, the makeup is fine, and maybe I'll try a few sips. But that," I point at the illicit baggie, "is way above my weight limit. I can talk my way out of being drunk if they find us up here, but I'll never explain away getting caught with illegal drugs."

"Fine," Pink huffs, rolling her eyes as if I'm a baby, handing me a tiny bottle of vodka. "Be a suck up your entire life, DD. It's definitely worked for you so far."

Did I mention Pink is actually meaner when she's fucked up?

She is, and that's part of why I don't trust the gesture of solidarity. That girl flips her switch like a complete psycho when substances remove her mask, and she doesn't give a single fuck who she splatters with her vengeance.

The rest of the Heathers snicker as they lay out the various sprays, brushes, and accouterments they plan on using on me. I sit on the bed with a sigh, carefully telling the story of my dress-capade, leaving out the parts that will get others in trouble if they get repeated. I don't want my misery to get Matilda or Growlvinchy in deep shit with my asshole parents. I never know what they're capable of, and Lucille, in particular, has proven me wrong many times.

Gold scurries over to the stereo, turning the music on full blast while I flinch. *What happened to the stealthy?*

She rolls her eyes at my reaction, slugging an airplane bottle of scotch. "Chill, DD. I guarantee they're passed out in their own corners by now."

"Definitely," Silver concurs, nodding as she shoots her own bottle while dancing around the room.

Shaking my head, I turn so Purple can tie my hair up in a high pony, sweeping all the strands off of my face. Something has been bothering me ever since Lucille made her pronouncement about the dress shopping. I can't wrap my head around it, so I decide to ask the girls to see if they think I'm being paranoid. "Do you guys think Lucille is trying to ruin the prom for me? If so, why? They *want* me to emerge, and it can't have escaped their notice that tons of preds do it on prom night."

"She's a bitch, DD. She doesn't *need* a reason. Crusty old cows like Lucille think they are far more relevant than they are, and younger preds threaten their power and their waning sexuality. They lash out at us because they see the end of their reign approaching," Pink remarks as she primps in the mirror. "They know we'll be at the top of the food chain soon enough."

There's a grain of logic in that, but I doubt B realizes it. She focuses more on flexing her power than being compassionate, and I'm reminded that Pink's viral video of her mother without makeup chased her off of every social media platform two years ago. Her gross 'Daddy' was pleased as punch, and her mother doesn't leave the house anymore. There wasn't a wrinkle on her face. She simply looked older than a fucking teenager, despite the years of high-end surgical augmentation. Pink did it because her mother had the audacity to ground her for a weekend when she got caught plagiarizing on an English paper.

The bribes it must have taken to keep her from getting expelled from Shifter Secondary had to be egregious. They don't actually *care* if you plagiarize when you're from an elite family—they care you got caught, and it tarnished their reputation. The Council families were terrified that allowing her to be booted would shine a light on *all* of us, and most of the teens from elite families definitely did *not* want that to happen. So it got swept under the rug, and it filled social media with brainwashed idiots chasing clout by defending her to their followers.

I was the only one in our group that wasn't worried about them looking through my papers. I don't cheat—at anything—so they were welcome to root through my life all they wanted. That infuriated Lucille, so Pink fucked up and I still got punished.

Story of my life, I fucking swear.

"DD, are you even *listening*?" Purple asks snidely as her brush dabs at my brows.

They're sitting on all sides of me like a swarm of piranhas, breathing booze and powder in my face. Each of them has brushes in their hands like X-Men claws and palettes balanced on their opposite palms as if I'm their own personal Sandra Dee. I can't see anything, but I assume I'm going to resemble one of the makeup tutorials on RipTok by the time they're done. I can feel the layers forming on my face, and it makes me cringe internally.

"Of course I am. Can you pass me another vodka?" Even though vodka is Lucille's favorite drink, I can't deny it's delicious.

"Fuck *yeah*, DD!" Gold grins toothily, turning to root in the bag.

For a brief second, I wonder why she didn't just grab a bottle from the pile on my bedspread, but I'm already a little tipsy from the first one, and the girls are buzzing like bees around my face. I take the one she gives me, downing it before telling the story of my parents' tantrum when I got home. It takes everything inside of me not to cry as I recount Lucille's awful words.

"Oh, poor baby!" Silver coos sympathetically as she adds more shadow to my right eye.

"I know," I mumble, shrugging. A hand smacks my shoulder at the movement, and I frown, but obediently hold still. "She's the absolute worst. She totally hates me. Who does that? Who *hates* their own kid?"

"Mmmm," Pink replies, applying solid blush with a blender. "I think my mom does, but who cares what that washed up old hag thinks?"

"Agreed," Gold adds. "My mother was the idiot who went careening off that cliff in a drunken stupor, so she's no better."

I say nothing in response. Gold's mother's case is still open, according to the Preynet. Most believe her father arranged it, as he quickly cut the brakes and replaced her mother with a *much* younger model. Even with the overwhelming evidence, Gold has never once uttered a word in her mother's defense.

Brainwashed—they're all brainwashed by the idea of power and money. They don't see the danger right in front of their noses, but I do. They're no less dispensable to their parents than I am, especially since they all have siblings, and I don't. I don't say that, though, because I'm just thankful they came over when I needed them.

"What are you guys doing to me?" I ask, suddenly feeling sleepy as hell and wondering when they'll get done messing with my face.

A husky chuckle tickles my ear as Pink adds more concealer under my eyes. "Nothing, DD. Just a fun new look. You'll love it."

I nod a tiny bit, my mind feeling fuzzy from the alcohol. "I trust you guys. This is a lot… more.. your.. thing… than mine."

"Exactly," Purple says, looking at me with an angelic smile. "Just close your eyes and let us work, dear."

Smiling, I sigh, closing my eyes to let my mind wander. Visions of the hot professors make my lips curl in pleasure, and the Heathers' voices get further away as scenarios featuring twins play through my head.

"...is she out?"

"Almost. What the fuck is making the Virgin DD smile like that?"

"Who knows? Maybe she's imagining Todd busting her cherry finally."

The laughter washes over me, but I ignore it, snuggling into the hot guy in my dreams.

"Look at her... such a naïve little twit."

"...have boned every pred in our group, even each other... the worst of us, and... hasn't figured it out..."

"She'll know tomorrow... I can't wait to see her face after... Hyenas are freaks."

"True, but high school dicks don't match their appetites... looking for college preds like those sexy ass professors... Tiny hyena cock isn't blowing my skirt up anymore; I don't know about you."

"Agreed."

"We're still going to meet them, though, right?"

"Fuck yes. Girls have needs, C... unlike double D's over there."

More snickers echo in the room, but my mind is too splintered to really comprehend everything I'm hearing. That vodka hit me like a ton of bricks, and I'm just gonna sleep it off right here.

Was that someone opening the window?

Will You Still Love Me?

Delores

"Delores! *Delores*! Wake up…"

The voice cuts through the cobwebs in my head, and I moan, rolling over to get away from whoever is shaking my shoulder. It's making me want to hurl, to be honest, and I can't even pry my eyes open to see which Heather is doing it.

"Delores! You *must* wake up; everyone has arrived and your mother is on the warpath!"

That gets my attention. The girls *never* call me Delores, and certainly don't care about Lucille's warpaths. The only person who would whisper so desperately is Matilda, and if she's here, I must have overslept my alarm by miles.

Why do I feel like my mouth is full of cotton balls? Gross.

I never understood how some prey animals can deal with furry little tails during sex, but I'm glad I likely won't have to worry about cutesy shit like that. With my luck, I'll be a dumbass wolf shifter—the most common pred around. I'm not anything special now, and I won't be then.

Ugh.

"I.. I don't... feel good, Mattie," I groan, flopping onto my back as the room spins. Clucking her tongue, she walks over to draw the curtains, and panic hits me. Where the shit are the Heathers? Did they get out before anyone came to find me? "Um…"

"Whatever you took last night to sleep must have been helpful, Delores. It's ten a.m. and even if you feel wretched, your team has arrived to get you ready for the dance at Apex tonight."

Blinking, I sit up, and the brass band in my head plays at full volume. "Took? Apex? Team?"

Matilda sighs and sits on the edge of the bed. Her voice drops to a more tolerable volume as she looks at me. "Yes, dear. They have moved the prom to Apex Academy because of some issue with the gym at Shifter Secondary. Lucille relayed that to me this morning, and I was supposed to tell you first thing. She also arranged for a team of stylists to assist with preparation, and according to her, it will take all day. She was so pleased with her intrusion that she didn't even open the boxes that came from Monsieur Growlvinchy —which is a good thing, I think."

My eyes fill with tears at my current predicament. The change of location ruined any plans I had for Todd and I after the prom, the vodka the Heathers brought left my body a mess, my friends left without a word, and now Lucille handpicked people to pluck and primp me to within an inch of my life.

I'll be lucky if I don't end up looking like an unpleasant episode of Drag Race.

Rubbing my hand over my makeup caked face, I croak, "Mattie, for the love of everything fangy, please find me some aspirin, a washcloth, and a plate full of grease. I can't deal with them all on an empty stomach."

Her face falls. "Delores, you're not allowed to eat before the dance

—Lucille's order. I'm supposed to lace you into the lingerie and corset, then bring you down to sit for them immediately."

Is she fucking kidding *me with this shit?!*

Not Mattie, of course, but my evil villain mother has constructed an entire day's worth of absolute torture to punish me for never living up to her expectations. This could be payback for many things, and I'm not sure if I'll make it. My belly is roiling, but even my inexperience tells me I should put *something* on it to help it settle.

"Okay," I whisper, giving in before Lucille sends someone worse than Mattie to fetch me. "But I at least have to have water and medicine. Then the punishment can begin."

"WHAT IN THE *HELL* IS *THAT*?" I GROWL, GLARING AT THE POOR woman wielding the smelly brushes with aplomb.

"Just lightening up the beautiful blond, sweetness," she mutters as she wraps foil around the sections of hair covered in the substance that's making me gag.

I know I seem like an idiot, but I've never done any of the high-maintenance shit Lucille wanted me to do with my appearance. I don't dye my hair; I shape my own brows, and I paint my own nails. She hates I don't avail myself of her generosity for beauty enhancements, but her dependence on a team of people to get her ready to even step out of her bedroom always seemed ridiculous.

Naturally, she has every type of service known to predator kind being performed on me today, making the hangover roar viciously through my system with no end in sight.

"It smells bad," I groan, closing my eyes. Maybe if I just let them work and drift off, I can figure out how to salvage my plans for tonight. If I can picture the grounds of the school, I toured the other day without envisioning the teacher hotties, that is. I have *no idea* why I'm so fixated on them when I have the world's best boyfriend locked down.

Something has to be wrong with me, right?

"Delores, sit up straight so you can get used to the corset. You must be able to breathe properly tonight so you don't pass out," Matilda chides from her perch at the window. She's been keeping a careful eye to ensure that Lucille isn't setting me up to look horrific, and I couldn't be more grateful, even if I can't show my appreciation in my current state.

"Ugh," I respond, my brain flitting back to holding the doorframe in the bathroom while Mattie pulled the stupid strings to tie me in like a heroine in a movie about the Old South. It felt like my ribs were re-arranging in my chest, and despite my protests, she pulled until my waist felt like it was in a sausage casing. "I was measured specifically for my dress. You don't think this will ruin it, do you?"

She shakes her head with a smile. "Monsieur Growlvinchy asked me before we left yesterday if I thought your mother would make you wear 'one of those archaic torture devices', and I told him I believed it to be likely. That's why the dress did not arrive until this morning right before you awakened."

My eyes pop open and I feel tears prick them. I don't know what I did to deserve Mattie or even this fairy godtiger fashion designer, but I'm so unused to anyone being this nice that it's making me feel like my heart is aching. "That was kind of you both."

"Dangerous, too," the peacock shifter in front of me mutters while she continues with my hair. "But I feel you. I hate how the predators try to make their kids feel like shit all the time. I promise we won't do anything to make you look bad, either."

Matilda smiles at her and puts her fingers to her lips. The rest of the stylist's team nods, agreeing to the secret pact we're all a part of now.

"Thank you," I whisper, looking at them all. "I don't know why I feel so hungover, but I'm sorry I'm not being helpful. My friends were over last night and I drank a bit of vodka, but I feel like a truck hit me."

"That's not what vodka and a hangover feel like, girl. Methinks you got bigger problems than just your momma," the brow wizard badger remarks. "Someone spiked the punch, if you know what I mean. You need to watch your back tonight... you seem to have more enemies than friends."

Seriously?! Did I break a sacred vase or something as a kid?

Now I have to worry about every single thing I eat or drink tonight while figuring out how to recreate my special plans with Todd in a new location that I'm not overly familiar with.

I hate my life.

By the time the crew finishes my hair, waxing, makeup, nails —along with getting me into the outfit—it's almost time for Todd and my friends to arrive.

I step in front of the full-length mirror, turning in place in my dangerously high heels. For the first time, I thank Hera that Lucille made me take a year of ballroom dancing as I'd break an ankle otherwise. I agree with the great Ginger Rogers—if I can dance backwards in heels, I can do anything. That's not *exactly* the quote, but it's close enough and I'm feeling a little more confident than I was in the boutique.

Monsieur Grrowlvinchy's dress clings to every curve, draping in the right places, and accentuating the curves Lucille hates so much. The added height of the shoes makes me look statue-esque, and the highlights in my hair make it shine like spun gold. Callisto, the peacock stylist, had her team pluck, tweeze, and highlight my face with a smoky chanteuse look from the days of ingenues and divas, so I look several years older than I am.

"You look beautiful, Delores," Mattie says, her face soft. "All grown up."

Biting my lower lip, I stare at myself again, finally rid of the effects of whatever the hell they dosed me with. All I want is for Todd to think I look beautiful and dance the night away together before we make love. If the universe could give me those few hours of happiness, I know I can survive whatever awaits me downstairs. "Thank you, Mattie."

She opens the door, and I walk out, straightening my spine and swallowing hard. I just have to make it through my parents' inspection until Todd and the others arrive with our limo to whisk me off like a princess in a fairytale. I can do this.

Before my foot even hits the top step, I hear Bruno bellowing in a scotch-filled snarl.

"*Delores*! Get down here so I can examine you before your date arrives. You will *not* embarrass us in front of all the families *and* the Apex staff tonight or so help me…"

He's already tanked and in a mood. Excellent. That means…

"Did your father stutter, Delores Diamond Drew?"

Yep, Lucille's in the bag, too. What a surprise. This is going to be ugly.

"I'm coming, Lucille," I call, starting down the stairs carefully. Dancing in heels is one thing, stairs are quite another.

Matilda rushes ahead, clearly hoping to placate them before I get down the marble staircase. I hear growls and snarls, the idea of them treating her so poorly making my empty stomach turn. When I finally reach the bottom, I stride into the drawing room. I'm shocked to find them in their usual corners, but with Bruiser holding a black briefcase besides scowling at me.

"Well, if it isn't the porky prima donna," Lucille mutters into her martini. "Getting you to look acceptable took four times as long as I take."

I steel my spine again, already prepared for her insults. I can't let her make me cry and ruin this gorgeous look Callisto and her team created. "I apologize, Lucille. They did quite a lot of work to make me presentable. Thank you for your generous gift."

She snorts, and my father walks over to Bruiser. He opens the case, revealing a starry sky full of sparkling jewelry pieces. I tilt my head, a confused look crossing my features. *Why does he have Lucille's jewels out of the vault?* I thought he was retrieving my small sweet sixteen set. No wonder she's saltier than a mermaid on a cracker.

"You will wear the pieces I select and if a single stone is damaged tonight, I will take the cost out of your hide," Bruno snarls, morphing into a half-shifted crocodile.

Shrinking back a step, I shake my head. "Oh, Father, I couldn't. That's far too... uh, kind. Those are..."

He cuts me off before I can finish my protest, stalking over with a gorgeous sapphire necklace. "I didn't ask, daughter. You will wear what I say and make certain any press photos of you at the dance include these pieces. I can't have the other families thinking we skimped out on your prom simply because you're such a disappointment."

I'm frozen in place as he snaps it on my neck, roughly adjusting it to sit exactly as it should. I don't want to be responsible for something of this value, and I'm certain Lucille will punish me simply for having it touch my worthless skin. But I murmur an appropriately grateful response, so he backs up and eyes me again. "Birdbrain, put the earrings on her. I can't stand being that close to failure long enough to deal with it."

My only ally in the room comes closer, attaching the matching earrings to my lobes gently, and I give her a terrified look that she reflects at me. Something about this stinks of a set-up, but neither of us will get me out of it.

The doorbell peels, and Bruiser grunts, snapping the case shut. Matilda scurries to the door, clearly hoping that it's my escape route.

If everything goes well tonight, maybe it will be.

Extra Lessons For The Unlucky

I despise this music.

Actually, I despise everything about what is currently happening in my home. The Tower is supposed to be my sanctuary—yes, laugh at the gargoyle having a sanctuary in a tower, everyone does—but I have been at Apex Academy so long that I've gathered an otherwise unwanted motley crew of fellow outcasts.

Aubrey was first, as he and I are the eldest shifters at the school and have a natural affinity. It devastated him when his clan cast him out for his youthful indiscretion, but he somehow found his way to my Tower. I wished not to be bothered, as I was mired in my own misfortunes after hundreds of years of moping. However, his quiet despair touched something inside of me I thought was long deceased, and I eventually allowed him to find refuge in my mostly fireproof home until he learned the control he sorely lacked. The dragon's anger has always fueled much of his inability to control his flames or to manage it more effectively.

Over the centuries, we fell into a companionable, if not grumpy, existence as friends and I learned to tolerate his eccentricities. After all, we are two of the rarest species of shifters—ones whose homes and families they ripped away with no warning—and it has always been unlikely that we would ever find another of our kind outside the kingdoms we no longer ruled.

But Aubrey's heart is even softer than my own, and when the trio of Khan outcasts showed up at the academy several years ago, he insisted we give them a chance. I still don't know what he sees in the clownish tiger twin—and the other keeps trying to play king— but the quiet artsy cheetah is amenable. Unfortunately, he is rarely without his adoptive brethren, and their inclusion in our friendship has caused more concessions on my part.

Like that blasted Slaystation…

"Renard, you're brooding again," Aubrey remarks, looking up from the laptop he has balanced on his lap.

He's sitting on one of the two specially constructed armchairs we had made for ourselves. Even in his human form, Aubrey is bulky, and though I am not, I love to be swallowed in a cushy chair when I'm not at my favored perch. Our chairs are situated close to my balcony, so that we can chat even when I'm soaking in the moonlight in my fully shifted form.

"I am not brooding, though I am consistently appalled at your poor choices in music, old friend."

The dragon belches, letting me know he's successfully hunted prey for the evening. I have not, as my typical dining choices do not emerge until darkness has fallen and I can fly off campus to find my meal. Dragons and gargoyles are very different predators than the muscle-heads in the other shifter groups, and neither of us prefers to chat with them about where we find our true sustenance.

"The thumping of the beat, the life in the sound... it calms the dragon. You know that." Aubrey pulls his glasses off and rubs his temples. "I need the inner Zen when I'm dealing with the rabbit holes I'm crawling into for Fitz."

Scoffing, I leap off of the balcony ledge and walk over to him. "It is a fool's errand. The Khan ambush has not been known for forgiveness, nor do they admit when they have done wrong. They have been ruling their fortress on Bloodstone with iron claws since long before our hardheaded friend was born. Out of all of us, I know the most about the rule he broke and how severe the elders of a species can be when they discover someone breaking their laws.

"Renard, my dude, you have got to let what happened to you go. We've been having this same conversation for centuries. It's what keeps you brooding up here like a giant bat…"

"Enough!" I roar, my temper slipping unintentionally. "I have shared many things with you, dragon, that I never intend to speak aloud again. The predators have excellent hearing, even when they are entranced by fighting games played at maximum volume."

Tiny puffs of smoke escape his lips as he clutches his stomach and laughs. "Rennie, man. It's *Super Smash Brothers*, and that's why I'm playing this song. You should try it sometime. I'm not as good as Chess, but I have to give the feline twins credit—it's hella fun."

Growling under my breath, I drop into my chair. "I do not think they made the controllers for beings such as us."

"That's why Fitz had special ones made—in bulk," Aubrey replies, rubbing the back of his neck. "I, uh, I may have a slight issue with not winning that occasionally results in controller damage."

I arch a brow. "Not winning? Is that what dragons call losing?" His eyes flash golden, and it's my turn to chuckle. "Always a sore spot, librarian. Pride goeth, the humans say."

"Oh, we're listening to those morons now? Please. Like I'm going to take advice from a species that thinks the lot of us are a bedtime story or movie plot. Besides, I don't like to chat with my food; do you?"

An outraged roar, a yowl, and a murmured sound cuts the answer I planned to give off. Sounds like Chess beat Felix again. The disgraced Raj hates to lose, and he can never seem to beat our mild-mannered cheetah. Fitz just sits there and mashes buttons to rile them both up. Their dynamic completely flabbergasts me, and I will never understand it. It goes against all the principles of what I know about their kind.

"That's why he always mains Meta Knight," Aubrey mutters as he studies something on his screen. "Oh, for fuck's sakes!"

Blinking at his outburst, I sit up in the chair. "What? What did that blinking box of doom tell you now?"

I hate computers, and I hate trying to use ones clearly not made for those of us who have been alive long enough to remember the elegance of written communication. But my scaly companion has adapted to the world much more readily than I, and he adores certain technology—when he's not destroying devices in a fit of rage.

"Avengers Assemble!" he yells over his shoulder with a glare. He turns back to me, huffing smoke like he's got a pipe in his mouth. "One of those idiots pissed off Henrietta; I know it. When I figure out who…"

"Five hundred on Fitz," I reply, slouching in my seat as annoyance fills my veins. As much as I have grown to care for the three of them, they get Aubrey and me in far more trouble than we ever found on our own during the last few centuries.

The felines straggle in, their expressions also filled with varying degrees of irritation, and I don't know if that's because of the interruption or one another. They take their chairs in the usual fashion. Felix leans forward with his elbows on his knees as he prepares to listen. Fitz drops into his indolently, flinging his legs over the arm like he's posing for Playgirl, and Chess sits with his legs pretzeled like a yogi.

The furious dragon slams his Smackbook shut, making Chess wince. I'm sure he's worried about having to replace it again—the custom keyboards cost a lot of favors from the cheetah's contacts in the Erickson family. Aubrey ignores him to stalk forward and snarl, "*Which. One. Of. You. Pissed. Henny. Off.*"

I snort at the nickname he gave the overworked and underpaid headmistress as I reply, "It wasn't me. I remain here unless I'm teaching or lecturing."

The three of them look at one another, communicating in some weird tiger way before looking at us with matching shrugs. Fitz looks as though he's hiding something, but he'll never admit it unless he wants to rub it in your face. The catalog of what he could have done to piss off a parent, a student, a council member or even one of the prospective students that were here last week is lengthy.

"Why are you having an inquisition?" I venture, hoping to help my friend before he truly loses his cool.

His eyes flash golden again, and he growls, shifting his shoulders to fight a half-shift. "Because they have *assigned us* to give a speech and chaperone a dance taking place on the grounds tonight for the incoming freshman from Shifter Secondary!"

"Are you fucking *kidding me?*"

Felix's outburst surprises no one, but I find the rest of their reactions quite interesting.

Of course, I want *nothing* to do with a bunch of horny, drunken teenagers dancing to raucous music and trying to paw each other to death in public. The last-minute planning irritated Aubrey. Normally, he'd be happy to give some long-winded speech about 'crossing the threshold to adulthood'. Fitz is almost licking his chops at the thought, and someone better remind him to check I.D. if he gets picked. Chess looks terrified, and he's hunched over, looking at his hands as if that will make it harder to see him.

Did something happen the other day during that tour? I only left my tower briefly to deal with the sea lions that dared to threaten the Captain and his crew, but I saw nothing out of the ordinary from my perch.

Fine. I have two sets of friends—my gang of outcasts and the raccoons. And maybe the capybaras that clean the tower. I'm also fond of the…

"We have to pick *two* of us to attend. I'm going to assume this is your fault." Aubrey glares at them. "Which means two of *you* need to go."

"Bullshit," Felix sneers. "*Fang, Claw, Fist*—like always. We didn't do shit."

"Outside of your ambush defiling my study room—again," Aubrey grumbles, turning to look at me. "Are you on board with the best two out of three?"

Rolling my eyes, I glare at all of them. "If I have to attend this, I'm kicking all of you out of here for a week. Keep that in mind." Quiet falls over the Tower and I smile in satisfaction.

Finally, the angry librarian clears his throat and sits, holding his large hand out. "All right. Are you ready?"

Determined looks cross the faces of each pred as they lean forward to focus. With each call of 'fang, claw, fist, BITE!', it becomes more obvious that they're avoiding beating me. It takes extreme self-control not to preen at the concession, but the truth is their teacher housing is terrible and Aubrey hates people in his library. They come here to avoid students and staff. We all have our own reasons for avoiding most of them, but this is our haven.

It was still my refuge first, and they'd better not forget it.

After two full rounds and two re-matches, the unlucky winners of a rubber chicken dinner and uncomfortable formalwear are Fitz and Aubrey. For a moment, I worry that the dragon inside of him is going to explode in fury, but he calms himself by turning the music back on. The others file off to resume their game, and I sigh as the blessed quiet during our mini-tournament gets broken by electronic music and shouted curses.

I hate all of it.

I had an enormous family and many friends in my clan before I was exiled. Until Aubrey arrived, I was alone for many years. It has taken me even more time than that to realize I didn't appreciate the support and companionship I had in the gargoyle clan. I lost one family, but throughout the years here, I found another. So even if I despise those things, I don't despise my family.

But they don't need to know that.

Don't Cha

I rush towards the door, ignoring Lucille's barked criticisms about being 'too eager'. Todd doesn't give a fuck about our stuffy parents' conventions, and I will not wait for someone to formally announce that the limo full of my friends has arrived to rescue me from the clutches of my DNA donors.

Matilda opens the door, and I stop short as I hear her gasp. My heels clack on the teak as I stop, unsure why the closest thing I have to a caregiver in this house of horrors has gone pale as a sheet. Her face turns to me, and my stomach clenches at the look of pity on it. Squaring my shoulders, I take a breath before striding over to her as she stands mute in the doorway.

Todd is leaning against the frame, the smell of cheap whiskey wafting from his rumpled tuxedo. His shirt is only half tucked in, and his hair is a mess. If that were the extent of the idiocy, I would get over it. But no… far worse surprises await in the background. My hand flies to my mouth, and I bite my lower lip hard to keep from ruining my makeup with the tears stinging my eyes.

The sleek, black limo isn't in the background as I'd imagined. Instead, there's an enormous bus with LED runners and blaring music. The shiny logo on the side proclaims 'The Landing Strip Party Bus', and the Heathers are hanging out the windows, waggling bottles of champagne at me. I can only assume the boys are in there as well, and by the sloshed look of my boyfriend, they've been riding around for a while before they came to get me.

"Delores," Matildas starts, but I wave my hand.

Nothing about this is fair, but very little in life is. I have to make the best of the hand that I'm dealt, or I'll never get away from Lucille and Bruno. Besides, getting smashed on prom night is a pretty common rite of passage, so maybe it looks worse than it is.

"It's okay," I whisper, passing her as I head out the door. "I'll have my phone just in case. Okay?"

She nods, pushing her glasses up as she stares at the neon monstrosity serving as my carriage to the most important night of my life. "Please be careful."

Nodding, I wait to ensure that neither of my parents is going to come charging across the threshold to laugh at my shame, and head out the door. I have no idea what possessed the boys to rent a party bus, but I'm sure it was Chaz's idea. That idiot is always talking Todd into doing stupid, thoughtless, or plain mean things, and this has to be his fault.

Gathering what little dignity I have left, I take Todd's arm to steady him as I walk toward the driveway with my head held high. I refuse to let anyone see how upset I am; they don't deserve my pain. Reaching the bus, I push my less-than-perfect boyfriend up the stairs by his ass, ignoring his drunken commentary. Once he's in, I turn to wave at Mattie and ascend the stairs.

I'm not ready for the sight that greets me. The driver lurches into gear and I grab the seats, holding on as both the movement and my disappointment nearly take my knees out from under me.

The Heathers are dressed in all of their designer finery—still coordinating by color—and they are obviously well on their way towards smashed. The boys are hooting and hollering from the bench seats as they watch Gold take her turn on the stripper pole in the middle of the aisle.

Yes, I said stripper pole.

She's shaking what Zeus gave her like she needs the money and the girls are shouting praise for her clumsy, intoxicated slip and slide around the pole. The boys are tossing hundreds at her, chugging cheap beer in tall cans. The entire scene is like something out of a bad teen movie, and it makes my hands shake in fists at my side.

This was not what I planned for the most important night of my life, and I'm furious.

I take a seat at the front, inspecting the surface before I sit. This gorgeous dress will have to be sprayed for biohazards tomorrow if the condition of the rest of the bus is any sign. Placing my hands on my lap, I sit ramrod straight, trying not to let the others see how this is affecting me. I don't know why they all did this, but I'm at the end of my rope. My mother tried to ruin my dress shopping experience and make me feel fat, my boyfriend allowed his friends to ruin our fairytale evening with a stripper bus, and my friends are so busy getting thrashed and pretending to be strippers they've barely noticed my existence.

My life is one big cosmic joke and I'm tired of being the punchline.

Todd stumbles over, holding out a bottle of Bacardi, and I shake my head. He pouts, but I don't relent. I can't get smashed—not with all of them barely able to walk. Someone has to be sober enough to get us from this monstrosity to the tables at the prom, and to be honest, I'd like to be the one *not* barfing on the way home—even if getting drunk would help me numb the pain of disappointment burning in my gut.

"DD, don't be such a stick in the mud," Purple calls, expertly swinging around the pole like she's done it a million times.

That figures. Her innocent, big eyed little girl act for her family's commercials has always been an act, but I don't think I realized until now just how much acting she did. She's definitely dancing like she's looking for a quick bang, and that's completely contrary to her public persona.

If only the faithful could see her now…

I shake my head to clear it. It won't help to push my anger at the situation into her. I'm not a slut shamer, and I firmly believe that women should be able to do whatever they choose with their bodies. Our world takes enough control away from us—particularly the Council heirs—and I won't allow my self-pity to make me a judgmental asshole.

Except we all promised to wait together.

Maybe the Heathers have been waiting until tonight to express their desires.. If that's the case, then I feel both guilty, and a little sad. They never told me they were feeling tied down by our pact, and I would never have held them back if they wanted to choose their own path.

Shit. Now I feel like an asshole. Way to be a feminist, Delores.

You hogtied your friends to some stubborn vengeance plot against your parents. They couldn't say no to it without upsetting you. Some 'body positive' feminist you are. You're as bad as the stupid adults ruling our lives like petty dictators at a chessboard.

I open my mouth to apologize when the bus slams to a stop. One of the Heathers tumbles off the pole and to the ground and my head whips around to glare at the driver. The badger at the wheel grunts, pulling out a flask and taking a large pull from it before he wipes his mouth on his sleeve.

Gross. Drunk driving a stripper bus to a prom—there's a life goal for you.

Closing my eyes, I call upon every ounce of patience and strength I possess as I stomp over to the pile of bodies and grab Todd's arm. He leers at me drunkenly, and I brace myself so I can yank him out of the tangle of limbs, pulling with all of my might. When he finally stands, I hook his arm around my shoulders and trudge to the front of the bus. We take the stairs at a glacial pace, and I don't wait for the others as I lead him to the small golf cart waiting to escort us from the main admissions building of Apex to the Arts and Humanities Center.

Once I situate the drunken oaf in the backseat of the golf cart, I climb in carefully, pulling up the bottom of my dress so it won't touch the floor. I have no idea how many people have been in this before we arrived or what state they were in. Underage drinking is common in the elite tiers of shifter society, and there's a decent chance there are students even more wasted than my companions already at the prom. They won't provide liquor to attendees, but they won't stop anyone who's imbibed from entering, either, because of who our parents are.

The scenery flies by as the driver tears across the lush grass and hills between the two buildings. He's short, with beady eyes and a slight frame that makes me think he's probably a smaller reptile or bird. It'd be rude to ask, but if he licks his lips at me one more time, I might heave despite being sober. I've never understood why men seem to get a pass to be legit creepers—even to younger shifters like me—and if I complained, someone would suggest it's my fault for wearing clothing that shows an inch of my skin.

I'm thankful that I found my future spouse early, so I didn't have to go through the meat market some elite girls have to go through to find their mates. Tonight, I'm going to solidify my dreams, even if the circumstances are not as perfect as I imagined. After all, real life is rarely perfect, and the lack of fairy tale romance I envisioned for this evening doesn't mean I'm wrong about Todd. It simply means I will need to figure out how to steer him away from his idiot friends once we get to Apex, so that he makes better decisions.

With that determined thought, I feel the golf cart stop and the Shirdal Arts Center sprawls before me. I wait until the other couples exit before I climb out and start maneuvering my boyfriend off the bench seat. He loops his arm around my shoulder and I sigh, half-dragging him towards the steps. It takes another five minutes to get him up the stone staircase, and though part of me wants to punch them all, I'm also relieved when I catch the shrill tones of Pink shouting into her phone from the golf cart pulling in behind us. She's probably recording an arrival video for her multi-platform empire because she's incapable of blowing her nose without using it to beg her followers to buy her line of shitty sex toys.

Did I forget to mention her sleazy father not only made his underage pred daughter the face of their media empire, but also the spokes model for their lingerie and 'personal care' lines?

I probably didn't, because it's creeped me out since we were freshman in high school and she started making videos about things I would never discuss with Bruno and Lucille. Their relationship is the ultimate full body shudder embodied in a dysfunctional corporation masquerading as a family.

The shrieking stops, and I turn my head, finding Gold looking as if she's ready to bite my face off for leaving them, and I'm in no mood for it. "Let's go, baby," I murmur, propelling my boyfriend to stumble inside with me.

Todd mutters something unintelligible and I sigh as we get checked in at the door. If we make it through dinner with no further incidents, I might even get this shitshow back on track. I just need to keep the rest of them from peer pressuring him, and we're golden.

***

"DD! DD!"

I look away from the Heathers holding court on the other side of our table to see Todd—now semi-recovered from his stupor— grinning like a madman and shouting my name. His boyish good looks make my heart soften a little, and I give him a fond smile. "Hey. Why do you look like the pred that cornered the prey?"

His grin is blinding, and I immediately forgive all the bullshit he's put me through tonight. I may have seen less of him this year with our classes diverging at SS, and the constant demands of our families' social schedule, but Todd may well be the reason I didn't lose it a long time ago.

It'd be really judgmental of me to not give him the same latitude he's always shown me. Maybe he just got caught up with his buddies and things spiraled before he realized what was happening. It's not like he'd ever *purposefully* hurt me by ruining our special night, right?

"Babe. Babe. *Guess* what I did!" He puffs up, his eyes still hazy from the booze.

"What did you do?" I reply, putting my chin in my hands as I lean forward to look up at him. Chad, Chaz, and Brett come running up, and I roll my eyes. Athena, save me with these morons.

"I spiked the punch!" Todd crows, holding up a rather large flask he's pulled out of gods knows where.

"Bullshit, dickhead! *I* spiked the punch," Brett growls, narrowing his eyes at my boyfriend combatively.

"No, *we* did!" Chad and Chaz shout, stepping closer.

Sitting up slowly, I rub my temples. Are they so goddess blessed stupid that all four boys separately spiked the giant trough of punch that every pred in here is gulping down like water? They can't all be that brainless—for the love of Dionysus, they just can't.

"Is… it possible… that none of you are lying?" I venture, looking from Todd to his growling pack of dipshits carefully.

Realization dawns on them slowly and they burst into a fit of snorts and sniggers, like children. Gold finally turns her attention to this side of the table, arching a perfectly sculpted brow. I shake my head and she shrugs, turning back to the lower preds who are fawning over the Heathers' dresses.

"*The Toddman's chick figured it out!*" Chaz yells, pumping his fist in the air.

I suck in a calming breath, closing my eyes before I snap at him. We've all gone to school together since we were babies and this idiot knows my name. That neither he nor any of the laughing fools acknowledge my place as Todd's future mate drives me batty, but I usually let it go. There's no need to ruffle feathers until my place is secure, right?

Fuck. That sounded a little too 'Lucille' for my taste.

"Well, hopefully, people don't get so blasted that they pass out before dancing." I squint at the program on the fancy flower arrangement on the table. "It says next they'll serve dessert while someone from Apex gives a speech."

Brett grins toothily, dropping into his chair again. "Can't wait to show whatever stodgy old fart they send what they're in for when we arrive next year."

Good luck to whatever poor professor they forced to give this speech. They're going to need it.

Respect

"I swear to Anubis, that asshole Raj has secret telepathy," I grumble. My hand squeezes the sparkly dragon squishy hidden in my pocket reflexively as I try to calm my nerves. Dragons are insular shifters—much like gargoyles—and speaking in front of sizable crowds outside of your family is unusual. I don't have large lectures like Felix or Fitz, and I'm not required to interact with students as closely as Chess or Renard.

This goddamned speech has me shaking in my fucking monkey suit.

Speaking of which, I look over at my erstwhile companion and huff as he practically skips his way to the Shirdal Arts Center. Fitz is unusually excited about attending a high school prom, despite it being an unpaid assignment outside of normal teaching hours. He's normally the first one storming into Henny's office to protest anything we're asked to do after four p.m. Yet tonight, he's effortlessly styled in his messy designer tux, whistling like a dwarf in a fairy tale as we head for a four-hour mandatory work detail.

I can't quite work it out in my head. This *should* cut into his 'slappy hour' with Chess or whatever female shifter is throwing herself at him this week. If Fitz isn't hanging in the tower annoying Renard, fucking someone, or with his ambush, it's not a day that ends in 'y'.

"Why so serious, lizard king?" he asks, making a face like the crazy villain in the confusing movie he made us watch about a man who is not a bat shifter, but dresses as a bat.

It takes everything inside of me to ignore his disrespect for my species, and I only do so because we're friends. Dragons are not mere *lizards*, and to suggest it would be a death sentence if I were any of the other members of my clan. "While I am uncomfortable with the situation, it is an honor to be asked to represent the school in front of the most powerful families in the country. I'm worried my lack of... social graces will be detrimental to our reputation. Plus, my history…"

The tiger stops moving entirely to burst out laughing; the mirth is shimmering off of him in waves as he coughs and sputters. I cross my arms over my chest, irritated at his humor at my expense. I don't often express feelings outside of anger, and my annoyance at his insensitive behavior makes the fire in my belly spark. Huffing a smoke ring as I try to regain control, I glare at him silently, waiting for him to explain himself before I turn him into a fried kitty steak.

When he finally catches his breath, Fitz tilts his head at me. "Listen, you big spicy iguana, this shit means *nothing*. We weren't asked to represent the school; they hogtied us into baby-sitting a bunch of baby council heirs. The Council members won't be at a kids' prom; hell, the school administrators won't be here. This is a punishment—probably for something or someone I don't remember doing—and nothing more. These little shits won't give a hairy rat's ass what your speech says—you could read the lyrics of *WAP* and they won't notice. Stop stressing; it's harshing the vibe."

Blinking, I open my mouth, and then I close it. It isn't often that Fitz says something so logical, nor often he thinks of anyone but himself or his brother. I think he may have tried to make me feel better in his goofy frat boy way. I'll be damned a second time. "You may be right, Fitzgerald, but it would not be right to shirk the responsibility I've been given, even if it is a punishment."

He snorts and rolls his eyes, reaching into his pocket and holding up a tiny baggie with the catnip strain of pred-stasy inside. "Suit yourself, scales. I plan on zoning out and chasing tail."

I let out a frustrated puff of smoke as he saunters off in his rumpled tux, whistling again as he goes. Leave it to that underhanded cheater Felix to stick me with his irresponsible party boy brother instead of someone calm like Chess or Renard. When I finally prove that he rigs our *Fang, Claw, Fist* games, I'm going to roast his goddamned chestnuts like it's Christmas.

"Fitz, wait! If you could refrain from taking that until I've finished my speech…"

But it's too late. He's raced up the steps and into the building before I can finish my sentence, and the little fun bag is empty.

This is going to be a fucking nightmare, and I'm going to murder the Khan brothers afterward.

"Your education at Apex Academy will be one of the finest in the world. Our Council families generously maintain the facilities to professional standards, and —"

"*Sucks!*"

A disembodied voice echoes from the back of the room, and my eyes narrow. If my entire speech goes like this, we'll all be lucky to escape the flames when I lose my shit. My hand squeezes the squishy dragon in my pocket as I work to maintain composure.

"As I was saying, they select our staff from many of the elite predator packs, clans, prowls, prides, and more so you will receive…"

"Blowjobs!"

Another voice, different from the last, joins in. This one sounds younger, so perhaps I can forgive their behavior since I know unemerged preds have poor impulse control. "You will receive a world class education, training in the arts and combat, and the wisdom of creatures years, and yes, centuries older than yourselves."

"Dragons are overgrown geckos!"

I am not fooled by my inability to see that heckler—the baritone in the voice is one of a grown ass shifter, not a child. My fellow teacher is near the back corner, and I now suspect he's encouraging these little assholes to interrupt. Whatever he was looking forward to tonight isn't happening fast enough for his liking—so he's bored and intent on stirring up his own entertainment. To make matters worse, he's got to be tripping fucking goat balls by now, and Fitz is ADHD enough *without* chemical assistance, so this is a train wreck waiting to happen.

Did I mention I'm going to reduce the tigers to cinders?

Clearing my throat, I continue, pretending his shenanigans aren't phasing me. "Apex is known for having some of the most skilled predators in the world on staff. We have alphas, betas, princes, princesses, and more roaming our halls as both students and professors. We will expose you to various subjects and fields of interest depending on what career you intend to pursue, and in your upper-classmen years, we will grant you permission to be an exchange student or intern with elite pred schools and institutions across the globe."

"Interns can suck my balls!"

My eyes close for a moment, and I try to get control of my temper. Fitz riling up the entitled morons in the back isn't helping, and I'm determined not to embarrass Henny or anyone else tonight. I take a sip of the water on the podium, hoping the cool liquid will quench my fire. Before I can open my mouth again to speak, a loud retching sound rings out in the middle of the crowd on the dance floor.

It's followed by another, and another, and another…

The room erupts into chaos as shrieks, puking noises, and the stench of vomit fill the air. Girls scream about saving their designer dresses as they scramble away from the students, who seem to aim for a Guinness World Record as their projectile bile shoots across the floor. Boys push each other trying to get away from the smell, sliding on the barf covering the floor and knocking over girls in heels. People crawl towards the tables, moaning and continuing to throw up as they go.

My eyes widen as I search the room for other adults to help. There's one lone girl sitting at a table, a frown marring her Fibonacci-perfect features as she watches the throng of students collapse into a vomitus wasteland. She doesn't look sick at all, and I can't help but wonder why that is. Her surprise is genuine, and I'm about to call out to her so she doesn't get sucked into the mess on the dance floor when a tiger roar distracts me.

Fitz catches my eyes, jerking his head at the doors and flapping his arms to show I should fly over the mess to meet him. Fucking great. He wants me to ruin my *one* tux to get the nurses for these rich fools. Son of a bitch, I don't know what I did to Ra this week, but he's clearly pissed.

I couldn't have had worse luck if I tried.

I strip the suit coat off to save it, letting my wings extend and shred the back of the perfectly tailored shirt underneath. Draping my coat over my arm, I rise slowly, hovering long enough in my half-shifted form to judge the ceiling height before I fly over the disgusting pit on the dance floor. When I land next to him, Fitz bobs his brows, his eyes glassy as he points at the gorgeous girl I noticed before.

"Pretty sure she saw my cock last week."

Pretty… what? For the love of Bastet, Fitzgerald Khan is not the brightest crayon in the box. Clearly, there are more important things going on than the pussy he apparently came to ogle. "Fitz, is that why you called me over here?"

"Fuck yeah, bro! She's got thighs you could smother yourself in. Chess and I…"

"*Fitz!*" I shout, my temper breaking free of its tethers. "There is a more pressing issue than your dick wagging at some underage pred. We have to get Bettina, Argyle, and Clarice right now. We don't know why these kids are sick, but imagine what will happen to us if any of these *heirs die!*"

Fitz's face goes white, and I know I've gotten through to him. The research he's asked me to do may never result in anything, but if we're the chaperones who let the Council heirs die, it won't matter that Felix is the rightful Khan leader. We'd be lucky if our deaths were quick. "Fucking shit, man! Where the hell is the prey staff housing again? They don't tell all of us you know—it causes staffing issues."

I roll my eyes. Of course, Henny can't tell most of the staff where they house hedgehogs, mongooses, pangolins, skunks, opossums, and the like—it would be a death sentence. This location is probably only shared with a sliver of the professors—trusted ones like Renard and I. "Forget that. I'll go get them, since they have venom resistance. *You* go to the infirmary and get their supplies. Tell that idiot driving the golf cart to fetch the nurses and to floor it or we're all going to get murdered."

He salutes me, shifting mid-air as he leaps, his clothes landing in a shredded heap on the ground.

Goddamnit. I fucking hate cats sometimes. Rich, idiotic, wasteful little shits drive me insane, and the Khan brothers were born and bred in the biggest pack of those fuckers.

I turn back to the ballroom, ripping off a piece of my ruined shirt to cover my face and muffle the stench. Moans, groans, and crying fill the air as I walk across the back of the room towards the buffet to examine the contents. My sense of smell isn't as good as Fitz's, but some poisons I should be able to scent on my own.

Just then, I see a flash of blonde, followed by a companion ducking out the sliding glass door that leads to the small patio area facing the lake. I don't know if I blame the girl for getting away from the rancid stench in here, but I find myself oddly sad that I won't get to speak to her. I was hoping to ask her what she *didn't* do tonight to determine why she's one of the few who aren't losing the contents of their stomachs on our parquet. If that led to more interesting conversation after, it would only be a delight.

But she's gone, spirited away into the moonlight like a fairy.

Fitz will be pissed, too. He seems to know her—if his dick comment was true—and she might even be the reason he accepted his fate so easily tonight. As if everything else going on at Apex isn't weird enough, Fitz might have a crush on an incoming student.

Oh, I'm going to get some mileage out of this for sure.

Can't Fight The Moonlight

Leaving the chaos of the prom disaster, Todd tugs on my hand as we exit the ballroom through the back door, leading me across the quaint little patio and onto the grass. The moon is shining brightly above, and the only noise is that of the nocturnal creatures around us. I look up at the stars, a small smile curving my lips. Tonight hasn't been all sunshine and roses, but as we stroll through the open space behind Shirdal, I feel a flicker of hope forming in my chest.

I know where we are thanks to my exploration at the open house, and my brows furrow briefly as my boyfriend continues to pull me away from the building and the lake nearby. We're headed toward the Shifter Training Area where I saw the primal fight last week. My cheeks flush as I remember the sculpted form of the tiger. I realized he must be related to the other professor I saw from the courtyard, because they are almost identical. Twins, maybe, and that thought has my skin heating even more. I saw a video once when the Heathers hacked the Wi-Fi at my house so we could check out Preyhub and—

"DD!"

A pair of fingers snap in my face and I blink, realizing I was fantasizing about the professors again. "Oh, sorry, baby. I guess I zoned out a little."

"We're here, babe," Todd replies, gesturing toward the wide, circular stone arena I peeped at last week. It's huge, and secluded, but the tang of blood that hangs over it speaks to the fights that regularly occur here. "Isn't this perfect?"

"Perfect?" I ask, looking around in puzzlement. "Perfect for what? Hanging out while they clean up the puke?"

A disbelieving snort escapes him and something uneasy settles in my gut. "To fuck. Duh."

"To... fuck?" I know I sound like a parrot, but after the bus and the scene inside, I'd kind of given up on the idea of losing my virginity on prom night. I didn't tell Todd about my change of plans, true, but when would I have had a chance? He's been drunk since before they picked me up, and after we got here, he spent his time clowning around with his boys. We haven't been alone for more than a few minutes all night.

Until now.

"Yeah. I mean, we've waited long enough, don't you think?" When I don't answer, he steps closer, taking my hands in his and squeezes. "I want to make love, baby."

I press my lips together, looking up at him. His expression is contrite, but something about this doesn't feel right. His soft brown eyes gaze into mine hopefully, but the uneasy feeling in my gut won't go away. "I do, too, Todd. I've wanted to for so long. Tonight has been a disaster—would it really be so bad to wait another day or two?"

His eyes darken, and I pull my hands out of his, taking a step back. A slow smile spreads over his countenance, and he edges closer to me again. Hands grip my shoulders firmly, and he leans in, whispering in my ear, "Baby, you make me so hard. I've been waiting for you so we can let our animals loose and get *wild*."

This is what I've wanted; it's what I planned for. The circumstances may be a little off tonight, but Todd's been more than patient. He waited when I first asked him to, and he's behaved like a gentleman about it ever since. I'm not saying that gives him the right to expect me to do something, but it shows what kind of person he is.

So why does this suddenly feel so wrong?

It must be the stress of the evening. Tonight has been a rapid-fire series of events I couldn't predict, much less control, and it has to be affecting my ability to see things clearly. Otherwise, I wouldn't be considering turning down my boyfriend of five years when he's professing his love for me.

Todd must sense the shift in my resolve because he puts his hand on my cheek, leaning forward to kiss me. The familiar scent and feel of my boyfriend fills my senses, and I put my hands on his shoulders, kissing him back until I'm breathless. He gives me that sweet, love-struck grin again, and my insides squish. Todd may not be perfect, but he's mine, and we are meant to be.

When we break apart, I push his tux jacket off of his shoulder, urging him to toss it aside. It goes flying, followed by his shirt, and suddenly, he's naked from the waist up. He isn't cut like the hot shifter professors, but he has broad shoulders and powerful arms. His muscles flex as he reaches up to brush a strand of hair off of my face.

"Turn, baby. I'll help you with your zipper."

The raspy tone of his voice makes my skin tingle, and I comply, closing my eyes when his hands work the hooks and zipper on the fancy gown. Slipping my arms out of the off-the-shoulder straps, I let the fabric slide down my body to the ground. It pools at my feet, and I instinctively put my hands over my breasts. I know we've been waiting for this for so long, but I'm feeling unsure and I don't know why.

"Todd, I…"

His hands squeeze my shoulders, and I feel his breath on my neck as he moves closer. "Relax, DD, it'll be over soon. Then you'll change, and everything we've dreamed of will come true when our animals mate."

I kick off the heels before I face him, my eyes wide as I take in his lanky frame. His lips curve up into a hungry expression and I shiver. Todd steps back again, undoing his belt and shedding his tux pants. My eyes track the skin as it's revealed before stopping at his boxer briefs. I frown in confusion, wondering if I'm doing something wrong, because I'm not seeing anything that looks like what I've seen lately… including in this training arena.

Monsieur Growlvinchy assured me this was the perfect lingerie set for this dress, both in form and function. So what's the problem?

Why does it seem like my boyfriend isn't even a bit… excited?

"Do you….do you like my…" I pause, a flush creeping up my neck. This is all so painfully awkward, and he's not doing anything to make me feel more secure. I lift my hands, spinning on the ball of my foot in a short pirouette. "Is this good?"

"Hell yeah, babe. It's hot as fuck. My dick is like steel," my boyfriend replies, yanking me against him. His mouth slants over mine, and I kiss him back, placing my arms around his neck.

I'm not sure I agree with the statement, but what do I really know? I mean, I watched those two hot guys get it on earlier in the week, and I saw the professor in the training ring, but seriously? It's not possible that every pred has a dick *that* big. The one who fought in this ring looked like he could rip me in half. Maybe it skewed my expectations.

Yeah, that has to be it.

Todd's hands skate over my breasts, tweaking my nipple hard through the sheer fabric of my strapless corset, and I wince. I've heard sometimes a little pain is sexy, but that felt like he was trying to remove a bolt. I squirm, hoping he'll get the hint and move on to places more likely to feel good when he's rough. At least, I hope it will. My barely there thong isn't drenched by any stretch of imagination, and if he shoves those tiny baby fingers in now, it will not feel good *at all*.

Maybe if I...

"Babe, touch me. Feel how crazy you make me."

Okay. That's a good idea. If I can get him worked up, he might return the favor, right?

Sliding my hands down his pecs, and over his abs, I frown. There's something... like little scars along them. The answer dawns on me as I keep my eyes trained downward and move my hands to his hip bones. My boyfriend is as vain as my friends—he's had ab implants!

The urge to giggle almost causes me to make this moment even more uncomfortable and I swallow hard, trying to avoid hurting his feelings. I can't imagine why he'd want to do that rather than some crunches, especially at our age.

But this is my mate, and I'm going to have to get used to the eccentricities I find as we learn one another's bodies. I wouldn't want him judging me for *not* getting enhanced, so I can't judge him for doing the opposite.

Can I?

My fingertips graze the waistband of his boxers as he continues fumbling around my lingerie, clearly having trouble with hooks and snaps. The groan he lets out encourages me, and I bite my lower lip as I slowly work them down over his hips to his thighs. Instead of a coarse patch of hair, I'm greeted with completely smooth skin, and yet again, I have to struggle not to laugh. I don't know if he had laser or if he does enough yoga to allow him to pretzel himself into shaving this close, but Todd Vandersnoot is as naked as a newborn below the waist.

Forget Hera, I'm going to need Aphrodite to get through this.

Movies and TV did *not* adequately prepare me for the tension, insecurity, and absolute shock I'm going through as I discover parts of my boyfriend's body I've never seen before.

I finally let my gaze travel past his stomach to the shallow 'v' of his pelvis, and my mouth opens in a perfect 'o.'

This is not what I expected at all.

"Yeah, babe. This is getting you all worked up, right?"

I'd been ignoring his lack of skill while I explored his body, but his fingers are fumbling around my lady parts like they've lost the map. I can't tell him if he's closer to putting a finger in my ass than he is to pinching my clit, and I also have no words for the sight in front of me. Reaching out, I clasp my hand around the base of his very short, thin cock, winging yet *another* prayer to the gods and goddesses that he's a…

What do they call it? A grower, not a shower?

Hell, I don't know. I zoned out for a third of the porn-fest the Heathers had in my room that fateful day, and I'm sincerely regretting it. Todd isn't doing anything to set my pussy on fire, and his equipment is so unimpressive compared to what I've seen lately that I wonder if I'll even feel it when he sticks it in. If he can figure out where to stick it in, because currently he's rubbing my taint like he's trying to erase a stubborn test bubble.

DD, you can do this. You're both inexperienced, and it won't be like this every time. Once you learn one another's bodies, you'll click, and you'll mate, and it will be perfect again. Don't hold Todd to unreasonable body standards; that's not your style.

If I keep saying it, maybe it'll be true.

"I want you," I lie, brushing my fingers over him lightly. That does the trick because he shudders and gives me a little push to show that I should lie on the ground. I bite my tongue as the thought of my ass on the ground is even less pleasant than most of my discoveries this evening.

When I hesitate, he rolls his eyes, and I swear he mutters something under his breath as he jogs off to grab his discarded suit jacket. I'm not going to lie—even hard, his tiny dick looks like one of those bobbing pool buoys as he runs. I'm not sure there's anything *less* sexy than every move he's made so far, but I'm not eager to find out.

Throwing the coat on the ground, he gives me another grin, though this time, there's a tinge of victory in his eyes that feels out of place. I drop to the ground, laying on my back, and he immediately sinks down to cover me. My thighs spread, and he settles between them—I think. It looks like that's what he's doing, at least. Todd glances up, his hand reaching over me to the flap of his jacket to pull a foil packet out.

"Gotta be safe, right? I don't want any whiny little brats keeping us from partying like rock stars when we own this place," he crows, wiggling his hips as he rolls the condom on.

I could tell him that Lucille made me get a birth control implant when I was twelve because I was 'so chubby and homely' that I'd probably let anyone stick it to me so I'd be more popular. I cried all the way to the doctor's office, in the office, during the procedure, and for days afterward. It's bad enough knowing you have no control over your life, but combining it with callous insults designed to cause insecurity makes it so much worse.

"Um… yes," I murmur. "We can't have that." I don't know *why* I just decided not to let him hop on bareback. It's not like I'm saving that experience for anyone, but it feels wrong and I'm tired of doing things that feel wrong simply because I'm supposed to.

A grunt and thrust later, Todd is inside of me, pumping his hips like he's trying to drive me into the ground. I hold on to his shoulders tightly as my body rebels against the dry prodding, and I wait for him to find the spot that will take my virginity and force my animal to emerge. It takes some creative maneuvering, but I finally tilt my hips just so, and the barrier rips. With a cry of pain, I clutch at him as he continues rutting for a few more moments, sweat dripping off his face onto mine.

The internet wasn't kidding when it said two virgins having sex is more like playing putt-putt than porn.

"Am I hurting you, baby?" he asks, his voice trying to achieve a growl but failing.

"N-no," I say, biting my lower lip and closing my eyes to keep the humor in them from offending him. I think I've had exams that were more invasive than his dick, but I sure as fuck can't tell him that. "Just like that, babe. Oh, I'm close."

Lies—all lies. I'm no closer than I was in the ballroom full of puke, but I need this to be over. I need my animal to emerge, and our mating to be solidified. Then I can figure out how I'm going to teach him what to do with a woman's body, even if I have to draw a damn diagram in crayon.

He breathes heavily at my words, and his hips jerk, his pained shudder letting me know something is finally happening. I let out a few breathy moans to ensure he believes I've climaxed, and he finally pulls out. His eyes find mine and he flashes a proud smirk as he rolls off and onto the grass beside me.

"And now, babe, we wait."

I look up into the moonlit sky and wing another prayer to Aphrodite, hoping that I emerge a bad ass pred who can finally take care of herself.

Bad Blood

Delores

Suddenly, a flash of pain wracks my body and my back arches off of the ground.

It feels like my entire skeleton is being both stretched and compacted at the same time. Panting, I stare up at the starry sky, my fingers digging into the dirt below as if I can hold on. Todd is saying something, but I can't actually make out the words because the agony in my frame is so intense that my ears are ringing. My eyes close and I wail as fire flows through my veins. The sensation of breaking bones and something spreading on my skin makes me cry out again, but there's no relief to be found.

Then, almost as soon as it started, it all stops and my body stills. I open my eyes, waiting for my vision to clear and sharpen as most predators do. But it doesn't—I can see on either side, but there's a blind spot in front of me. I move my head back and forth, trying to figure out how this works, when a loud exclamation nearly deafens me. The clanging in my skull is only rivaled by the intense thumping of my heart as it beats faster than I have ever felt before in my life. My back left leg twitches, thumping the ground as I glance around wildly. The shouting is coming from Todd, who I can see now that I've re-positioned my head.

"You—You—*You!*" he screeches again, the sound making my ears ache with its pitch and volume.

I can't respond—no shifted preds can, except a very few gifted alphas with superior genes—but I thump my foot in frustration again to get his attention. My body is shaking with fear, and despite Todd's *many* flaws, I don't know why I would respond to him this way. The trembling is so intense that I can't seem to control it and it makes my nose itch. Instead, he points an accusatory finger my way, his eyes flashing yellow for a moment as he spits on the ground next to me. My heart rate jumps again and the instinct to flee flows through me like lava from a volcano.

Danger, danger!

"I should *have known* you'd be some measly half-breed! Making me wait all this time, like a fucking monk only to put out for a *lousy, inexperienced* virgin lay," Todd growls, pacing in front of me. "My father said it was a good match, and we'd be rich and powerful, but look at the Drews *now*. They produced motherfucking *prey*."

His words sink in, and I realize that every single thing I've been feeling since the change is *not* what any pred should be feeling. The fear, the pounding blood, the instinct to run—those are *prey* reactions. *Holy goddamned shit, I'm not a predator. Oh, my goddess Hera… he'll kill me.* I have to go; I have to get away before his change finishes and I'm dinner. My legs decide to work for more than a feeble Morse code and I leap into the air, taking off into the bushes to get away from whatever hungry predator Todd is.

He's destroyed me—completely broken my heart and soul—but staying alive takes precedence over that. I don't even know how to shift back yet, and I definitely can't defend myself in whatever form I've taken. It feels tiny, and I don't hear my animal's voice inside of me yet. I read online that it takes time to hear it, and all I know right now is that I *have* to get to safety.

"I'm going to ruin you, Delores Drew. You can run, but you can't hide. You stole five years of my life while I waited for you to grow up and claim the power our animals give us. I sat through every stupid date and listened to every dumb wedding fantasy. All I wanted you to do was give it up so I could secure the marriage agreement between our fathers. But, oh no, not you. Unlike the rest of us, Saint DD of the big tits refused to *lower* herself and emerge. Well, look at you now—you're food, and the rest of us are going to eat you *alive*."

A pathetically weak howl echoes through the training area and I realize Todd has just shifted *without* the pain I experienced. Large paws appear outside of the bushes I'm concealed in, and I hear a weird giggling sound before he takes off into the night, the sound as deafening as thundering hooves to my sensitive ears.

Shifting that quickly can only mean one thing—he didn't wait. He's been cheating on me, and he's had his animal for a while, possibly even the entire time we've been dating. Another wave of betrayal washes over me and I ache from head to toe as the realization that my life has been a lie lances through my soul. As if my animal can sense the torment inside of me, pain shoots through my body again, and before I know it, I'm lying naked on the grass in the bushes in my human form, panting as I stare up into the night sky again.

How?! I want to scream into the Universe.

My parents and grandparents are preds from long lines of predators—we have DNA maps. There's no way this could be happening. Yet, the instincts and bodily functions I felt when my shift emerged were *not* those of any Apex pred, not even a small one. It seems impossible, but Todd's expression was so disgusted, hungry, and full of outrage there's no way his reaction was a prank. Whatever sort of four-legged predator he is—I didn't get a clear look at him to see which—the truth was revealed during his fury.

My intended fiancé didn't wait for our perfect prom night as he promised. There would have been no reason for the limo, the champagne, the rose petals or the fancy suite, even before they moved the prom to Apex. Everything I knew about my life—from my boyfriend and friends to my lineage—was an illusion.

They all tricked me and now I'm humiliated.

Sighing heavily, I gather myself enough to roll to my feet and plod over to the gown I loved so much. All the glitter and style seem dulled in the wake of my revelations. I ignore the corset and torn undergarments—Todd ripped them off because he was too uncoordinated to figure them out—and simply slide myself into the dress. With some flexible yoga-style moves, I zip the dress enough to keep my boobs—the ones he sneered about—covered. I reach down and dangle the shoes off of my fingers because they are beautiful, but I'm not wearing them for my walk of shame across campus. I can't deal with teetering on soft grass along with everything else.

It occurs to me that the jewelry Bruno made certain I wear is nowhere to be seen. The necklace and earrings must have dropped when I shifted and had to flee from Todd. That's another thousand pound weight on my shoulders because it may not be the first thing I get in trouble for when I get home, but you can bet it's going to come back to bite me. Lucille is going to lose the fucking plot, but there's no way I can crawl around the training circle in the dark to find the blue stones. Not now, anyway.

I'm not crying yet. It's like there's a block on my emotions. I know a giant, uncontrollable wave of rage and pain is coming, but it's sitting on my chest like a thousand pound weight. My body is running on autopilot as I trudge back towards the Shirdal Arts Center and whatever fresh hell awaits me there.

I can't sneak around the front because the door monitors checked everyone in when we arrived. I don't want them to realize I didn't stay in the ballroom like we were supposed to. They're probably still attending to the sick preds, so it's possible I can sneak in through the back and slip out the front door to find a place to hide until I can call Mattie to check me out when she picks me up.

When I reach the back door, I open it quietly, tip-toeing into the chaos. There are three nurses in pajamas—a hedgehog, an opossum, and a mongoose—attending to the students one by one. The stuffy dragon that eyeballed me is standing in the corner, half-shifted, with huge iridescent wings tucked against his back. They're beautiful, and I wish I had the time to go over and see them up close, but I can't risk it. He looks concerned, but also like he's trying to find someone and is annoyed that he can't. I avoid catching his gaze—it looked like he wanted to question me earlier and I don't want to draw any more attention to myself.

My back presses against the wall of the room, clinging to shadows as best I can while I slink towards the front entrance to the ballroom. If I can make the next forty feet without being noticed, I'll be home free. I just hope that Todd hasn't—

"Look everyone!"

I freeze as the sound of Pink echoes through the room like knives on a chalkboard.

*"It's DD, the big-breasted **bunny shifter**! Shall we show her what we do to prey at Apex Academy?"*

My head turns and I look at her standing on a chair with her phone at the ready, clearly live streaming this for her RipTok. The other Heathers follow suit, climbing onto chairs and baring canine fangs at me. Gold wiggles her fingers at me and blows a kiss before turning into a wolf. Purple crosses her arms over her chest, arches a brow, then morphs into an African wild dog. Silver snaps her jaws, shifts into a coyote, then looks down at the boys below as if waiting. They've all half-shifted into hyenas, including Todd.

My friends lied.

Every. Single. One. Of. Them.

The devastation sinks in for a second before self-preservation kicks in. I have to go. I have to get out of here *now* and hide where they can't find me.

If I don't…

"*Run, rabbit, run!*" someone screams gleefully.

Pink looks down and smirks. "Give her a little head start, boys. The Pred-pros you're wearing will livestream the chase and her last moments directly to my channel. I'm hoping for a billion views by morning, so make it bloody."

She just ordered them to kill me on live TV.

Fuck!

Clutching my shoes, I hike the dress up and run like hell out of the ballroom and front door, almost tumbling down the steps of the building. When I get to the bottom, I look around in a panic before I remember the secret courtyard in the library I discovered last week. It's enclosed enough that my scent might not draw them while masking me in the leftover pheromones of the hot professors.

I take off like a shot, hearing the train of my dress rip and the expensive shoes clack in my grasp as my feet pound the grass between Shirdal and the Draconis library. If I don't make it, I'm going to die after the lousiest lay in predkind, and that really pisses me off. Gulping in huge breaths, I push my limbs to the max, almost leaping up the stairs of the library. The doors are open and I thank Athena, figuring she's the most likely to be protecting my post-virginity scorned ass.

The halls are pitch black, so I have to pause for a brief second to allow my vision to adjust. Once they do, I picture the route I took to get to the main library doors, and then the steps I wandered along that took me to the little oasis amid cement and metal. When I finally find the door, I sigh in relief when it swings open without catching on a lock.

I suppose being a school full of predators makes you less likely to believe you need extra security to protect things.

Stepping onto the cool grass, I drop the shoes and reach down to rip the remains of the long train off my dress. It is definitely ruined—much like me—and I can't stand to be contained any longer. The ragged hem now falls loosely above my knees and I climb onto the stone table on the right side of the tree. My legs criss-cross, and I briefly consider that I might flash someone, but given that I'm probably the only prey on campus hiding from ex-friends who want to eat me, I'll take the risk.

I go to pull out my phone and realize it was tucked into the secret pocket of my corset, and I left that in the training arena.

Hera above, what in the literal fuck *am I going to do now?*

The dam breaks and the tears come, the absolute futility of my situation hitting me in the chest like a baseball bat.

I'm all alone and I'm going to die.

She's Put A Spell On Me

Fitz

Nothing like a bunch of teens blowing chunks all over themselves to ruin a decent buzz.

Aubrey's snarly commands were impossible to ignore, especially since he put a little of that 'alpha shifter' shit behind them. Dragons aren't called that—as he loves to remind me—but as the second-in-command to my Raj, the push of a true royal still affects me. My laced nip was wearing off, thank Bast, so I understood my friend's implication that they could blame us for this crap because they forced us to be chaperones.

Listen to a bunch of rich fuckwits whine about their precious heirs' safety in some dumbass tribunal? *No fucking thank you.*

I shifted and hauled ass to the infirmary as instructed, even letting the damn prey animals hitch a ride back so it'd be faster. Knowing I was that close to food without eating it is making my skin itch, but I have better control over my cat than that.

Luckily, the grumpy librarian didn't seem set on me staying behind to help him coordinate the clean-up. I suppose I might have if asked, but since he didn't, I grabbed my shit and headed out into air that doesn't reek of vomit. If Felix had been with us, he would have ordered me to help and since he's the only being on the planet I answer to, I wouldn't be strolling along the grass untouched by sick high school kids.

Nice.

My ears flick when I pick up a faint noise coming from the direction of the library. Frowning, I alter my course, hoping I won't find a sick kid I have to escort back to the puke palace. When I approach the building, I realize the sound is coming from the courtyard where I saw the gorgeous girl last week. My heartbeat speeds up—I couldn't be this lucky twice, could I?

Creeping up to the dark alcove, I use my tiger's eyes to see better. It wouldn't do to get lured here for a beat down from a salty ex or some choad who lost to me in the ring. You can't trust anyone in a snake pit like Apex and the sooner new arrivals figure that out, the longer they last—students and staff included.

When I get a few feet from the sound, I realize I should leave an offering somewhere because the gods are smiling on me for the first time in a while. The hot blond who sat here and pretended not to watch Chess and me explode is curled up on the stone altar like a fucking sacrifice.

Forgive me, Ra, for I have sinned…

I grin to myself at my dirty joke, then approach the edge of the grass quietly. If my luck holds, she won't be heaving like her classmates. That would force me to do something adult-ish like take her to the nurses, and the last thing my dick wants me to be is responsible right now. My vision narrows as I notice she seems to be ragged and I can't figure out if that's some stupid fashion designer's idea of edgy or not.

Like I keep up with that shit. That's Chess' job.

"Are you okay?" I ask softly. I don't want to scare her, but that's exactly what happens. She shoots up like someone bit her, clutching the weird dress to her chest and scrambling backwards. I hold my hands up in surrender, then add, "If you need them, the nurses are giving out medicine for the stomach thing in the arts center... I can take you?"

Her expression fills with terror and she shakes her head. "No, no, no! Don't make me go back there!"

A flashback of something that happened when we were cubs hits me, and I recognize her behavior immediately.

Someone hurt this girl and when I find them, I'm going to peel their hides from their body.

The realization that I'm dangerously angry over a girl I don't even have a name for makes me confused. Sure, I'm a decent dude, but I stay out of people's shit unless it affects the people I care about. It's not that I don't care as much as I've learned that trusting anyone not in my personal ambush leads to pain and trouble. Everyone else can get fucked is almost my life motto.

As much as I wouldn't give a damn if this rich chick got dumped normally, something about this doesn't feel right. Her scared tears are making something writhe in my gut and I can't put my finger on it. The threat tumbled from my lips without pause, though, and despite my love of violence, I don't offer to kill preds for merely upsetting someone.

Unless it's Chess.

That thought disturbs the hell out of me, so I go back to focusing on the weeping blond on the altar. I step closer and she rears back so quickly she almost falls off the stone. Her reaction puzzles me; I wasn't being threatening at all. Why would she be acting like I'm going to hurt her unless...

My eyes narrow as I tilt my head and scent the air. The jasmine from the tree fills my nostrils first, but then I catch it. A slight tang of blood and the scent of...

Holy feathered eagle balls. It can't be.

This Council heir must smell like prey because of all the scurrying animals in the ballroom. There's no way one of them is hiding a kid set to inherit their throne who isn't at the very top of our food chain. The scandal would rock the foundations hard enough that even I'd hear about it.

Besides, I know I couldn't smell her animal when I saw her in the gym, and that means she was a virgin. Though with blood in the air now... perhaps that's changed. Is that why she's acting like I'm going to rip her throat out?

Motherfucker, I'll kill...

I take a deep breath and shake my head to clear it. Calm down, Fitz, you're going to scare her more. If one of those idiot boys hurt her, she's not going to trust a male simply because he's a professor. We had some weird seminar about this last year and though I slept through most of it, I vaguely remember how they described victim behavior.

"Hey. Listen," I try saying again. "I won't make you go anywhere you don't want to. But I feel you're not okay, and I can't just leave you like this."

"The puking is because Todd and his idiot friends spiked the punch," she spits out. Her face changes when she says the name like it's distasteful, which sets off alarm bells in my head. She swipes at the tears, then wipes her nose on her tattered dress with a huff.

I don't know what the hell they spiked my party favors with, but suddenly, I want nothing more than to hold this girl in my arms and tell her everything will be okay.

That's ridiculous, of course, because it's almost never true.

"Is Todd why you're so upset?" I observe her face because her response is going to sentence that asswipe to a painful death if it's affirmative.

Her eyes widen and more tears spill out as she lifts her hand to cover the whimper that comes out of her mouth. "He... We... I'm..."

Fury flares in my soul and my fangs drop as I snarl, "Did he force you? Did that motherfucker rape you, baby girl?"

She shrinks away, obviously terrified of my response, and I have a stern conversation with my tiger until he pulls the pointies back. Once I do, she's able to meet my gaze again. I give her a sheepish look, rubbing the back of my neck as I search for the right words.

It's not like she knows I saw the bruises and smelled sex on her.

"I won't hurt you; I promise. But I need you to tell me what happened because it's very hard to control a tiger when it's angry."

Her lips curve a little, but I consider it a win. Her voice is barely a whisper when she replies, "I know you won't hurt me. And... he didn't... rape me. Todd was supposed to be my fiancé but... now... Things didn't go as planned and I'm sure that's off because my whole life has been a lie."

Shifting from foot to foot, I argue with myself for a moment before I gesture to the other side of the flat stone. "Can I sit?"

The girl chews her bottom lip for a moment and I have to talk the other monster down before I do something stupid as hell. By the time she nods, I'm pretty sure I won't embarrass myself when I sit that close, so I join her. I say nothing at first because I'm not sure how much I want to share, but I want her to feel better.

"I can relate to life not turning out how you expected. You may not realize it, but no matter what they spin to the students, most of the professors here are not here by choice. Something in our lives happened, and we got sent here as punishment."

"Really?" she looks up at me wide eyed and I have to swallow a groan.

"Really. When new professors get here, they take a while to adjust because most of us are fucking furious that we're stuck here teaching rich brats. Even if we're former rich brats ourselves." I smirk a little and she ducks her head, so that I don't see her trying not to laugh.

"Why do you stay? You're adults, right?"

Oh, to be young and this naïve again.

"We are, but that doesn't mean our choices aren't limited. They would kill some of us if we left, but all the exiles have nowhere else to go where they can be around their people. And maybe some of them are punishing themselves for getting sent here."

Felix is one of those. I suggested we make a break for it after the first year, but he refused. My stubborn twin doesn't even like me doing research to overturn my father's decision. He spends most of his time denying himself everything possible in penance: touch, his hair, friends, sex… you name it.

But it's not in a Khan's nature to submit and I won't unless he directly orders me to—which I know Felix realizes.

"What if you could go back but everyone is going to treat you like shit over something you had no control over? Would you do it?"

"That's a very specific hypothetical, baby girl." I smile crookedly and shrug. "I guess it would depend on if I thought I was strong enough to look them in the eye and say 'get fucked'. If I knew I could do it, I would make sure they knew they can't break me."

Lifting her head, she looks me straight in the eye. I see a spark of sass there, almost like a pre-cursor to anger. "I haven't let them break me yet."

"Don't start now," I counter. She straightens, pulling the remains of her dress over her with a determined look, and I grimace. No fucking way can I let her wander around like this. I reach down and pull my shirt off, holding it out to her before I continue.

"They can knock you down, but they only win if you don't get up."

My dick damn near does backflips when she pulls the shirt over her head and it covers her perky tits. I really should get an award for this shit. The guys will never believe I haven't hit on her even once. Even Chessie will be impressed.

"Be patient and play the long game," I tell her. "Let them think they've won, but gather your resources and your people. You need people who you know would fight to the death for you and will never be turned. When you have that, you can make a plan to make them all pay for fucking you over... but not before. You know only the vicious survive in this world, baby girl."

The blond watches me with big eyes and a little awe as I rant. She's chewing on a stupidly long fake fingernail as I talk, and I can't tell if she's inspired or trying to get the nails off. I thought I gave a hell of 'rah-rah' speech, but who knows what girls need to go all 'boss bitch' anymore? Maybe I should have looked for fucking Zhenga or something...

"That's really helpful, Professor..."

Oh, hell no. That's not happening now.

"Fitz. You should call me Fitz. None of that formal bullshit, eh?" I give her an amiable smile, hoping I don't look as dopey as I sound. "Do you need to use my phone? You seem to have lost..."

"Everything?" she trills a soft laugh and delight fills me from head to toe. "Yes, that would be very kind of you... Fitz."

I'm going to hear her say my name in that husky voice every time I fall asleep from now on, for fuck's sake.

I hand it to her, unlocking it and staring out into the night as she calls someone she refers to as Mattie and arranges a ride. Clearly, she doesn't want to go anywhere near the people she came with and given her current state; I prefer it. Hell, if she hadn't gotten a ride with this call, I might have offered to take her my damn self.

Chess is never letting me live this shit down when he hears about it.

"Should I stay with you? I don't want you to feel unsafe, baby girl."

She tilts her head, then shakes it. "No, I think I'm okay. Mattie is picking me up here at the library and we have a code where she honks, so I know it's her. Plus, you've been far too kind already. I can't thank you enough for talking with me."

I'm not sure I can leave her here without making certain she's not in danger, but I'm great at hiding behind things to stalk prey. She doesn't have to know I'm watching and then she won't feel bad. "Okay. Just remember what I said, baby girl."

I rise, winking as I move to leave, but then she calls out, "Why are you calling me baby girl? You just said I'm an adult."

My lips twist and I arch a brow at her. "Because you were in this courtyard last week, dolled up like an e-girl, while you watched me and my consort fuck against that window. All you needed to be hotter was a tiny baby doll tee."

Her eyes widen and her cheeks flush bright pink at my words. "Oh."

I shrug and wink at her. "Maybe when you come here in the Fall, you can see another performance."

"Mmmm, I don't know if that will work," she says with a mischievous grin. "Your… friend… got really aggressive and skittish when he gave me that tour of the art building. I'm not sure if he likes me."

My brow furrows. What tour? Chess didn't even mention that to me.

I don't have time to respond when she talks again. "Plus, I don't know if I'll be coming here after all. Something happened and well… even if I do, I won't last long."

"No one at this school will lay a finger on you or I'll cut it off, followed by less pleasant appendages. Count on it," I snarl, flashing a fang again.

She shrugs, unperturbed by my tiger now. "We'll see, Fitz. Good night."

Frowning, I wave at her, then turn to head out of the alcove towards the staff housing area. I don't enjoy leaving her, but I'm also weirded out by Chess not telling me about their encounter. Plus, I just acted like a psycho older dude stalker and I'm not sure how I feel about that. Everything about tonight has been clown shoes and I'm not ready for the damn circus..

Or maybe I am, because I didn't even ask her fucking name.

That's okay. I know a pretty good hacker.

Me—I'm talking about me.

Mean

Delores

It's crystal clear I can't depend on riding back with Todd in the ho-wagon. Even if he was still my boyfriend and the Heathers were still my friends, popular kids run in a mini-pack formation. Until this calms down, they're going to shun me, or worse. I'll have to deal with all of my heartache and grief alone.

That's okay—it won't be the first time and definitely not the last. Our world is pred eat pred, and they expect all of us to learn how to survive on our own if we have to. Lucille and Bruno haven't failed in that aspect of my upbringing at all. I certainly know how to take care of myself because no one else gives a rat's ass about me except Mattie.

The ride to the house is silent, and I'm thankful for it. I'm terrified of what awaits me when I get home because I know by now, Pink will have broadcasted my shame on every social media platform available. There's no way they have not made my parents aware that I'm a bigger disappointment than they expected.

I'm the lowest of the low, the unworthiest of unworthy... I'm prey.

After she arrived at the library in her tiny sports coupe, Mattie located my phone. She has an app on her tablet that allows her to find any of our devices in case of theft or kidnapping. I was a little shocked when she said the second part so matter-of-factly, but I guess it's a precaution our family's security team would have taken to ensure my father didn't have to pay out a hefty ransom. I waited in the parked car while she retrieved it, nervous for her safety given that I was well aware of what kind of preds are stalking the grounds looking for me.

My parents will be furious, of course. I've humiliated them by emerging as a peasant in our society and they captured my embarrassing run for my life for the entire world to watch. I destroyed my dress, messed up my face, and they ripped my heart to shreds. I'll be lucky if I survive the night with what's left of my soul intact.

No one makes Lucille look foolish and lives to tell the tale.

They may make good on their threat to send me to Bloodstone Isle, or they may simply disown me. If that happens, I'm going to need to learn to take care of myself in ways I've never had to before. I have a little money saved from pocketing the change when my parents gave me cash for purchases, but not enough to find a safe place to stay for very long. My credit card is certain to be cut off, and I'll have to carry everything I want to save on my back, since I won't have a car.

Sniffling, I wipe a tear from my eye as I think of how Todd and my friends betrayed me. That's the biggest lesson of the day, I suppose. You can't trust anyone, and everyone is always looking out for themselves. It doesn't matter how perfect you try to be or how well you behave, nothing is ever good enough for those who want to tear you down.

Everyone who I thought cared about me—save Mattie—falls into that category today. They didn't want to hear my side of the story or comfort me. They just wanted to attack and further their own goals. I should have expected it, and I'm a fool for being so damn naïve.

'I'm young' is a convenient excuse, but the real problem is my inability to accept the truth that Lucille kept trying to drill into my head. She pulled no punches about the cut-throat nature of preds and frequently told me I was being silly and sentimental. I just thought she was being a mean old hag and tried harder to get her to love me. Maybe it is my fault for being too naïve. I should have listened, even when it hurt my heart to do so.

She's never liked Todd. I guess she was right about him, too.

The car pulls up to the front steps, and Mattie finally turns to me, her eyes full of sadness. Her voice is a whisper as she says, "Are you ready?"

"No," I reply, shaking my head slowly. "But I never will be and if I'm going to die tonight, I might as well get it over with."

A look of horror crosses her features, and I give her a watery smile before I get out of the car to head to my judgement.

There really is nothing else left to do besides face the music.

"*How* did you let that little *slut* Barrington film this *disaster?*" Lucille shrieks as she paces back and forth across the drawing room in satin pajamas. "*I cannot* believe her father *refuses* to take it down. If this is his idea of a power play…"

I watch her with dull eyes, makeup trailing over my face as the tears freely fall. Between her and Bruno ranting, I've been standing in my ripped dress and bare feet for two hours now. They've threatened, ranted, and cajoled many people over the phone as they frantically work to get the videos removed. When they're on hold, they scream at me or… worse.

The broken glass count is up to ten, and that's *after* Matilda cleaned up the first set and brought a fresh tray in. I've ducked most of them, but it's difficult because Bruiser steps closer as a warning every time I try to move from the spot I'm standing in.

Bruno hasn't come close to unleashing any of his typical alcohol-induced threats, but it's coming.

If they can't make headway with the 'fixers' they have on the phones, my night is going to get much, much worse. My punishments get more violent when the stakes are higher, and though it's not all the time, it's difficult to predict which face my parents will show.

My heart is thumping like a brass band and I can feel my entire body trembling. Biting my lower lip so hard I taste blood, I struggle to keep myself under control so I don't give them any more weapons to use against me. But it's getting harder by the second, because now that I've emerged, my animal is *much* closer to my skin.

I'm prey, being stalked by threatening predators. The bunny inside is fucking terrified, and I can't hear her yet—that skill comes with time and training—so I can't soothe her with mental conversation. My nails bite into my palms as I try to replace fear with pain, to keep my scent from alerting my parents about my dilemma.

"M-may I g-g-go up s-s-stairs?" I venture, making myself as small as possible. I can't keep my voice from shaking, but I can try like hell to get out of here before the rabbit flashes over my skin.

"We are not through with you yet, Delores Diamond Drew," Lucille purrs, her eyes dark as she half-shifts and her fangs come out, causing another wave of panic to shoot through my veins. "I always knew you were a useless fraud, and you'd never amount to anything. I carried you, supported you, and yes, *put up* with you because I thought someday I might get rid of you through a marriage agreement. Now, that's impossible because you had the audacity to turn out so flawed that even my pull can't save you."

Flinching, I lower my head and look at the floor. Lucille has no compassion for emotions, and no use for weaklings. If she knows how badly she's sliced my already fragile self-worth, she'll go in for the kill.

I can't break down here. I have to remain as put together and contrite as possible, even though I know I'm not to blame for my animal emerging the way it did. DNA and genetics determine that detail and I could point a finger right back at Lucille and have a fifty percent chance of finding who was responsible. One of *them* knows the truth, but they will never admit it. The root of my parents' problem is staring at them in the mirror, but they seem more interested in blaming me for being caught on video.

"*Oliver Barrington...* if you do not do something *immediately*, I will call our *mutual friend*s and we will see just how big those shriveled old man balls of yours are. Do you think a shark out of water can defend himself against the tigers? No? Then I suggest you put a muzzle on that little tramp and call me when it's fixed. You have *two hours*, comrade. After that, our friendship ends, and who knows what will befall you?"

Lucille hangs up the phone, chucking it across the room like a missile. I wasn't watching carefully enough, so it hits me in the face hard enough that I can *feel* the bruise forming. Her anger is like a living thing, filling the room and suffocating all of us as she seethes. I don't move for fear she will fully shift and come after me. What if my bunny appears? I'm not sure my mother's in a state of mind that will allow her to make any sort of rational decision if that were to happen.

The cops are in her pocket, so if she killed me, she'd never see a courtroom.

Bruno hangs up as well, turning to face us from where he's been sitting, muttering things to one of his contacts. His eyes glitter with rage as he advances on me slowly. The gator inside of him shimmers over his skin as he stalks towards me with the fury of a predator who has lost their prey. "Well, well, my little... snack. It seems the Council believes it would be better for us to allow you to live... for now. They think your death at Apex—whether at the hands of a student or in the battles—will reflect better on the school and the Council. After all, who wouldn't want to send their pred to a school where even an heir can die at the hand of the most vicious?"

My eyes widen and I tremble, shaking my head wordlessly. Both of my parents give me supremely satisfied grins, and even Bruiser snorts his approval. Mattie wrings her hands in the corner, looking like she's going to be ill. This has to be a joke—one colossal joke played by the gods to pay me back for all the times I defied my parents in little ways.

They can't actually be sending me to Apex—a school of elite predators—as prey? One glance at the faces of my parents confirms I'm not imagining things, and they really are sentencing me to death by my classmates.

Cowards—the lot of them. They should kill me themselves if they want me dead.

I won't give them the satisfaction of knowing they broke the last piece of my soul, though. They don't deserve to feel good about their destruction, and I'm not yet ready to fight back, like the professor, Fitz, suggested. So I nod, turning on my heel and running up the stairs as fast as I can. I have to lock myself in my room so I can finally, finally let it all out. After that, I can plan what I'm going to do to keep myself safe.

IT. WON'T. STOP. BUZZING.

I set my phone to silent once I stripped my dress off and tossed it in the garbage can. Unfortunately, I made the mistake of unlocking it to check the time, and the messages started pouring in like a tidal wave of pain and betrayal. My ex-friends and ex-boyfriend filled every social media platform from Instagrowl to Riptok with vile comments, death threats, and laughter at my expense.

I should report the things people said as online bullying, but who am I going to report it to?

Pink's video went viral long before Lucille's threats to her dad made him take action. It's been shared so many times that no one can stop it now. To make it worse, Todd decided to doxx me, so I'm also getting regular texts full of hate on top of the social media threats.

I'm a little worried people will show up at my house, but I don't think they could get past Bruiser's security team. He might not care if I die, but he won't let anything happen to my parents. They've killed staff for less, and he knows it.

No one has come to find me since I ran to my bedroom, and truthfully, I'm glad. Even seeing Mattie right now would make my shredded heart ache. How could I have known when I woke up this morning that my entire future would disappear like a puff of smoke? Not that I could have done much to escape my fate. You can't change who you are.

All I can do now is lay here in my room and cry, and hope that I'll be able to pick up the pieces tomorrow. I'm friendless, loveless, and futureless, but at least I'm not homeless or dead.

Yet.

Sympathy For The Devil

Fitz has been taunting Aubrey about the now infamous 'Vom Prom' for days. After he delivered the medical staff, the beleaguered dragon lost the one sober witness he claimed to see, shredded his shirt, and got vomit on his favorite shoes. We've listened to him bitch ad nauseam and I'm going to lose my temper if my twin doesn't stop baiting him.

"You survived, you old grouch! I know you hate leaving your trash can to deal with people, but you aren't dead."

I look over at my brother, deciding I might live without him if he gets the dragon going again.

"The library is hardly a trash can, Fitzgerald, though sometimes I wonder if it's a brothel because of you." His lips curl up as he narrows his gaze on my lazing twin. "I do not appreciate your disrespect regarding my library or the safety of the students."

"You're laser focused on this chick, lizard man. Feels like you're less concerned with finding out why she wasn't sick and more like you have a great big dragon woody for her," Fitz drawls with a smug grin.

"I know why she wasn't sick, you dipshit. She didn't drink that nasty punch. And you shouldn't even be speaking of her!" Aubrey jumps to his feet, advancing on my brother with a dark look that makes Chess shrink back. "She was as pristine as porcelain, her golden hair glowing in the lights like a seraphim. Not once did she look sweaty or ashen, like the rest of the students. Her features were perfect: a testament to Fibonacci's ratio if I've ever seen one!"

What's gotten up the lizard king's ass today?

"Fibonacci was an uptight prick," Renard mutters from his perch on the balcony.

I'd ask, but the gargoyle isn't one to elaborate and I'm not sure I really want to know.

Fitz, however, is nonplussed. Aubrey's outburst doesn't ruffle him because he was trying to piss the dragon off. He turns to Chess, grinning broadly. "You realize he's talking about the baby girl we saw in the courtyard, right?"

The cheetah turns red and stammers, "Oh? I didn't know she was here again. I almost forgot about it, to tell the truth."

My brother lets out a derisive snort as he stares at his consort. "Uh-huh. Sure you did, baby."

Fuck, Fitz, is it really the time to pick a fight, especially one you don't want to win?

"We should find out if the nurses know what they added to the punch and why it made everyone sick." I look at the huffy dragon expectantly. "Have you spoken to them yet, Aubrey?"

I don't want any of them to realize how angry I am. My tiger is pissed as fuck that someone infiltrated our home and tried to harm people we're responsible for. Not only did they get past the school defenses and security, but they flew under the radar of all the preds employed here as well. It makes us all look like incompetent fools.

Especially my brother and the dragon king I sent to represent us.

Apex Academy is our home now. None of us have lands to defend or people to rule, but this was a direct challenge to all authority on campus, including the higher tier exiles like myself. The four people I care about most in the world are in this room and depending on what the poison was, it could have harmed them, too.

This is more than just making snooty Council kids toss their cookies at a dance.

It's defiance and I won't stand for it.

"Felix. Felix, stop. Hey, bro. Calm down," Fitz says.

Blinking, I look down at my hand where my claws are digging into the arms of my large armchair. Shit. "Sorry," I mutter.

My twin is in front of me in a blink, pressing his cheek to mine in a soothing gesture. When my tiger settles, he pulls back and grins. "I may have more intel to share. Some cockrocket named Todd spiked the punch, so if we can find out what he and his fellow douchenozzles were drinking, we can rule something out."

"That would help us determine why that alcohol neutralized the poison's effects enough to only cause vomiting!" Aubrey gives me a begrudgingly pleased look as he re-settles on his throne. "Do you want to locate him, or should I?"

Fitz gives him a shrug, but I can see the wheels turning in my brother's head. "You do it, man. I have another project to work on."

What the fuck is up with him and that girl?

I chuckle as Aubrey pulls out his phone and starts stabbing at it with a muttered curse. Looking down at Fitz, I ruffle my hand over his hair. "Where did you get this info? You know, I enjoy hearing about your methods of squeezing intel out of people."

"I just asked her, man. It's not like I need to beat on a chick," Fitz says, looking uncomfortable. "Unlike Señor Firepants over there, I found her on prom night."

Every one of us stare at my twin as if he's grown a third head.

"When did this happen?" Aubrey and Chess blurt at almost the same time.

Fitz winks at Chess, ignoring Aubrey so he can needle the cheetah. "I thought you'd all but forgotten her?"

"Stop," I growl in warning. We need to work together, not provoke one another if we're going to identify the threat to our home. I don't mind Fitz giving them shit when it's not serious, but now isn't the time to divide us to amuse himself.

Waiting until Fitz submits, I sigh and let go of his hair. "Aubrey is tracking the Council heirs. We'll find out who they are so we can pay them a visit this summer when everyone is far away from their schools and most of the parents have fucked off to their summer homes."

"That's a good idea, Felix," Chess says softly. "Obviously, most of them aren't as powerful as Khans, but we don't want to draw unwanted attention. Also, I'd prefer if no one got hurt by an overzealous bodyguard."

"I won't allow anyone to be harmed, Chess," I reply on a rumble.

Renard snorts from the balcony, but not everyone has rocky armor like him.

"Oh, save me, Mr. Growly Tiger King," Aubrey says as he looks up from his phone with a smirk.

That makes Fitz snarl and his white tiger ripples under his skin as he looks at the dragon mocking me. Aubrey simply smirks, his eyes turning iridescent as scales appear and disappear at will on his bare skin. It's a not-so-subtle reminder that his beast could swallow all of us whole and not even get indigestion, and I don't miss it.

And Bast help us if the damn gargoyle joins him.

"We may poke fun, but you are correct, my tiger friend." I almost jump out of my chair when the silent gargoyle actually speaks. "For all we know, the Council themselves are behind this."

His suggestion sucks the playfulness out of the room, and we all look at one another in apprehension. Being exiles, we don't give a fuck about them unless they specifically come for us, but every other shifter at the school is under their rule. People who piss off the Council usually get sent to Bloodstone—not poisoned at their crown jewel school.

"Why would they do this and put their own heirs at risk? Seems like a dumb plan," I say as I scratch my chin.

His eyes are pitch black as he looks at us. "I watch things. There-fore, I see more than most. In the many years I've been at Apex, I have never seen so many potential targets in one place. The bulk of the kids here are heirs or have ties to them. We should find this Todd, but it's unlikely he did anything but make a lucky mistake. Something of this scale feels like a larger plot aimed at much bigger prey."

Who is bigger than the Council and their heirs?

"I'm going after the moron myself," Fitz growls as he rolls to his feet and walks over to sit with Chess. "I have unfinished business with him."

Frowning, I look at him as he snuggles Chess and buries his face in his neck. Fitz is rarely ever this worked up over a chick. He's almost protective, and that only extends to our ambush. This silly girl, a Council heir, has wrapped him around her finger and I don't have a clue how she did it.

Courtesans and queens have tried to entice my brother, but he fucks them and moves on.

We're in big trouble.

This Is Me

"Fuck *all* of this!" I shout, digging my fingers into my hair as the anger and hurt wash over me again.

Picking up the Alexa on my nightstand, I heave it at the mirror on my dresser as hard as I can. The glass shatters, and I pant as I stare at the destruction from across the room. My reflection is as shattered as my soul, and I can't find it in me to give a damn.

I've been locked in my room for two days. It's not exactly solitary confinement, but the one time I opened the door, Bruiser threateningly glared at me from across the hall, so I retreated. Trays of food appear every so often, and I eat as much as I can stomach. I haven't heard from Mattie, and I haven't seen my parents. My phone's battery nearly exploded from the heat as the messages, texts, and videos continued to roll in. I've quit looking at it; I leave it plugged in on the carpet so I can't hear it vibrate.

My fate is hanging by a thread, and I'm not involved in the decisions—as usual. Life as an heir has always had elements of helplessness and a ton of unfair expectations, but I tried to play the game. I did what they asked of me; I wore what I was told, and I assumed the role with as much grace as I could muster. Clearly, my efforts didn't matter, because everyone cast me aside the minute I didn't fit their precious mold. Fury roars through my veins as I think about all the times Lucille cut me down for her own amusement—all the times I simply took her abuse, hoping to win her approval.

Realization trickles into my consciousness slowly. The Heathers never supported me when I struggled; they shrugged it off as 'how things are' and talked about themselves. Gold is the one who came up with my nickname, and I thought it made me one of them. But Todd's harsh words from the shifter ring echo in my mind. DD was always an insult, not a pet name. He and his buddies played into it constantly, so they had to know Gold was making fun of me.

Nothing in my life was ever real. It was all a carefully crafted illusion created by people who wanted something from me: a pawn to control, a quick fuck, prestige. None of them ever gave a damn about me—hell, Todd's boys barely even remembered my nickname, much less my real name. They all lied to me about their animals emerging; that was clear in the quick shifting they did at the pukey prom.

Looking at my splintered reflection in the mirror again, I surge to my feet and stomp over to the dresser, enraged by what I see. My body isn't my own—I spent hours in the gym to keep my figure as close to their standards as possible so no one would force me to get enhanced. My makeup and nails match the current trends in *Sassy Pred*. I have perfect hair, perfect teeth, and perfect clothes. Others have shaped everything I am. I couldn't control the cosmic twist that erased all of my hard work and sacrifices anymore than I could control anything else.

If that's how it's going to be, why am I bothering? Why am I sitting in this room eating when I'm told, hiding like they want, and being the perfect plastic doll they've demanded? Doing so hasn't changed the outcome of this mess, and it certainly will not keep them from sending me to Apex to be killed.

What in the hell does it matter if I go off the rails?

Hell, people will probably expect it. I'm ruined, right? Don't all disgraced teen socialites go on a bender after their humiliation?

I can get away with damned near *anything*, and it wouldn't be abnormal at all. A complete makeover, booze, pills, tattoos, piercings… god forbid, I might even dye my hair! None of it would be unusual for a poor little rich girl with emotional trauma.

A vicious smile creeps over my face, making a portion of the weight crushing my chest lift. Delores Drew has never shown who she is—not once in her whole life—outside of dance lessons. The things I love and hate, my hope and dreams, fears and failures were all cloaked under the mask of the obedient Council heir. They don't have a clue what they've done.

Death is not a threat hanging over my head anymore; it's a certainty.

I'm free.

The Council and my parents made sure I understood what outcome they were hoping for by sending me to Apex next year despite my… situation. My only chance at survival is to do what the sexy tiger said and let them think they've won. I won't fight them if they decide to keep me out of the public eye for the rest of the year, not even if I have to miss graduation. I'll take classes online to finish school, and I'll spend the rest of my time in my room—planning.

Their gambit puts not only *me* in chains—it restricts their behavior as well. Regardless of whatever PR spin my parents' team puts on the situation, they have to pretend nothing is wrong until I get to Apex or this scheme falls apart.

That means they can't actually kill me, or have me never show up in public, because people will be watching. Neither Lucille nor Bruno will want reporters camped out at our house, recording their every move for long. It would interfere with their crooked bullshit and affairs.

Once the fervor dies down, I can defy them in ways I never could before.

That thought is the first glimmer of hope I've had since I played confessional with Fitz at Apex, and I laugh through the tears streaming down my face. He's right; I might be on the mat now, but I will not stay down. I have three months to learn who I am, plan for my enemies' comeuppance, and find a new family who accepts me for who I am. It will take a lot of reflection, and a lot of heartache, but I have to do it. I need to discover the Delores I would have become if I hadn't submitted to these expectations since childhood.

My eyes flit to my phone and I scramble over to it. Fixing my Airpods in my ears, I let the music from my 'In Another Life' playlist wash over me, helping me focus on existing rather than aching. When my eyes are no longer leaking tears, I clear all the hateful notifications from my lock screen with a decisive swipe. Even though I'm trembling, I block numbers from my call list, and after that, I open each social media app and block every asshole until the taunting numbers on the icons disappear.

Once that's done, I sniff again, noting my contacts are fairly sparse now, but that's okay. Every house is built on a foundation, and the new Delores will be as well. It will take time to gather up the pieces of my heart and soul that were shattered last night, and even longer to glue them back together, but it will be worth it to rebuild myself in an image that I love—one that is actually me.

I won't allow anyone else's opinion to decide my fate ever again.

⬩

WHEN I PEEK OUT INTO THE HALLWAY THE NEXT MORNING FOR MY breakfast tray, I'm shocked to find Bruiser missing. I take advantage of his absence to slip out to the gazebo with a croissant, my phone, and a pad of paper.

As I scroll through the paired down names and apps, I remember a few whispered words from my dress shopping excursion, and another tiny grin creeps to my lips. The lightbulb goes off in my head, and I almost cackle in satisfaction when I realize how much this plan will piss off… well, everyone.

I shoot a quick text to my potential ally, hoping the answer I get is affirmative. If it is, I can use the funds I earn to save for my escape. The cachet will keep Lucille from forbidding me from doing it, and the status will give my ex-friends the finger in public —bonus.

No wonder people like this rebellion thing so much. It feels like a mini-orgasm when you imagine how angry the haters will be when they find out they haven't won. I think I like it—a lot. In fact, I might just stick with it. I mean, being a good girl hasn't done me any favors, right?

If you can't join 'em, fuck 'em.

It's time I put on my big bunny panties and show them what I'm capable of. Todd can tell everyone I was a shitty lay on Instagrowl, the Heathers can shun me on Riptok, and my parents can forbid me from leaving the grounds until the press goes away, but none of them can stop me from dusting off my ass and standing my ground. I can take the punches and ask for more; I know I can.

They didn't like the obedient, proper Saint DD*?*

Fine. She's a ghost.

Lifting my pen, the first thing I do is make a list of every single one of their offenses. Once I'm done, I realize I have to play the long game if I'm going to get them back for everything they've done to me—Lucille alone has enough major violations to keep an entire revenge department busy—so I need to pair this down to the most heinous crimes. A girl's gotta have priorities and I'm going to be busy keeping myself alive as well.

Next, I make a shorter list that I can keep on me at all times, just in case I need to shore up resolve when I'm struggling or if I'm sad. Then, I add a sassy title, because I can.

Fuck 'Em Up, Sis List

Lucille (existing, shaming me, throwing fucking glasses at me, calling me fat)
Bruno (threatening to send me to Bloodstone, fists, plus Bruiser)
Todd (lying, cheating, hunting me, shitty sex)
Heather E. (nicknaming me DD, being a twat, dosing me)
Heather B. (videos, sleazy dad, ordering my execution)
Heather H. (liar, behavior on stripper bus, hypocrite)
Heather C. (follower, didn't help me)
Chaz, Chad, Brett (not knowing my name, hunting me, stripper bus)
Anyone else who gets in my damn way.

Sighing in satisfaction, I fold the list into tiny squares to fit in my bra. No one's getting their grubby hands in *there* soon, anyway. Plus, it's much less likely to be found, just in case someone snoops through my belongings or fucking frisks me.

I might be a little paranoid, but I'm justified. People are trying to kill me or get me killed, and they aren't even pretending otherwise. I have to stay on my toes or I won't live long enough to burn this place to the fucking ground and victoriously bask in the flames.

They may see me as prey now, but the most dangerous predator is a woman scorned with nothing left to lose.

GET THE NEXT BOOK, LET US PREY NOW!

WORLD GUIDE & PRONUNCIATIONS

CHARACTERS

Delores Diamond Drew (duh LOR es DIE mond Droo)

Lucille Rostoff Drew (lou SEAL ross TOV Droo) leopard, evil genius, Dolly's mother

Bruno Drew (Brew noh Droo)- crocodile, Dolly's father

Matilda/Mattie (mahTILduh/ mahTEE) Lucille's assistant, former nanny to Dolly, hawk shifter

Bruiser (Brew ZER)- komodo dragon, bodyguard for Drews

Heather Erickson (heh THUR AIR ick sun) aka Gold, bitchy ex-BFF, wolf

Heather Barrington (heh THUR BEAR ing tun) aka Pink, bitchy ex-BFF, jackal

Todd Birkshire (doosh BAHG)- hyena, former fiance to Dolly, asswad who took her v-card

Fitzgerald Khan/Fitz (FIH TZ jair uhl duh/ FIH TZ KAH N)- comp sci, Pred Games, tiger

Felix Khan (FEE licks KAH N)- professor Shifter Studies 200, tiger, twin of Fitz, exiled heir

Chester Khan (CHeh SS KAH N)- Apex Student Liaison, Guidance Assistant, cheetah, Fitz's consort and mate

Aubrey Draconis (AW BREE Drah CON iss)- Librarian and Archivist, National Library, exiled King, dragon

Renard Laveaux (Rey NAR d LA Voh)- Guest Lecturer at Capital and the Smithsonian, exiled King, gargoyle

Rufus McCoy (Roo fuss MICK OY)- honey badger, gangster, heir to drug empire

Cori Bouvier (kor E boo VEE ay) polar bear

The Captain- pirate raccoon, heads crew, loyal to Renard

Luc Growlvinchy (looKUH GR owl VAHN she) Dolly's boss at design firm, (tiger)

Emile (ee MEAL) pangolin, head of pangolins who work for Growlvinchy

Zhenga Leonidas (zen GUH lee oh nEYE diss)- shifter biology and Pred Games

Heather Honeywell (heh THUR hun EE wel) aka Silver

Heather Charles (heh THUR ch ARRL zuh) aka Purple

Henrietta Shirdal (hen REE ett UH SHEER dahl)

Betsy (behT see) ostrich; library aide

Professor Cormac (kore MAHK) English department; platypus shifter

LOCATIONS

Apex Academy - college being repaired from magical bomb incident

Drew Mansion- Delores' home

House of Growlvinchy- designer fashion house she worked at

Khan Battle & Training Arena- training arena

Bloodstone Isle- Khans rule this island and reform school

Honeywell Admissions Building- cafeteria in here

Shirdal/Shird- Arts building

Townhouse- Tiger ambush staff housing

Draconis Library- where Aubrey works and archives are

Leonidas Gym

Shirdal Theater- where they perform

Cambridge- nearby large city

The Tower- where Renard lives (among others)

Cambridge- nearby large city

The Tower- where Renard lives (among others)

Reviews, Print, and Merchandise

If you have enjoyed this story, please review it.
It helps other readers find my work,
which helps me as an indie author.

Thank you!

Reviews are appreciated on the following platforms

TikTok
Instagram
Facebook
Bookbub
StoryGraph
Threads

To purchase print copies or merchandise, go to The Worlds of Cassandra Featherstone

GET A SECRET BONUS SCENE!

For a secret bonus scene that follows *Come Out & Prey, click the link below, sign up for my newsletter, and get your freebie.*

Get your bonus scene here!

Sneak Peek: Bloodthirsty

QUEEN BEE

They dim the lights in the club, and the spots click on as the curtain slides open.

It's a full house tonight in the little burlesque club off the Rue Pierre Montaine.

Chez Arc En Ciel is not well known compared to the *Moulin Rouge* or *Le Lido*, but the wealthy from both sides of the Seine gather here for shows four nights a week. If you pass the various layers of security checks to even be permitted to book a reservation, you also have to be able to afford the two thousand Euro per guest cover charge. If you don't eat or drink anything, that's all it will cost; however, that would get you blacklisted.

Intro music pumps through the speakers and I stand on my mark in the opening position. My cane is resting on the wooden boards of the stage by my front foot as I pretend to lean on it. Roars of applause echo through the room as our troupe of dancers catch the lights, sequins sparkling like diamonds when the stage lights rise. We're dressed in pinstriped black pant suits and fedoras to match the big band style opening to the song. As soon as the horn-filled intro finishes, the dance begins.

I follow the routine with precision, snapping and popping my hips to the beat as we spread out across the stage. You wouldn't know by the fake smile on my face that I'm scanning the crowd. Two fan kicks later, I've rotated past the proscenium, and I think I've found my mark. Twirling, I stop in the place I need to be for the bridge, singing along as if my life depends on it. It might, to be honest, because I need to sell my cover tonight, so no one notices me.

The Guillotine moves in the shadows, but tonight, she's in the spotlight.

My ass shakes as I dance my way through the song, swinging the prop cane I'd replaced with one of my design. You wouldn't know by looking at it, but it's not the painted balsa the other dancers have for a very specific reason. I need it to complete the mission that forced me to spend two months in Paris working my way into this job at *Chez Arc En Ciel*. If I can't strike tonight, the surveillance, counterintelligence, and time spent building this cover are wasted because my mark is leaving for Asia tomorrow.

Tonight, the Cobra dies for his sins.

The break of the song slows the music and the dancers pour into the crowd to wiggle around the rich assholes. It's choreographed, but it's also to advertise each girl for private dances in the lounges upstairs. We're not strippers—not that there's a damned thing wrong with a woman using her body to support herself—but we do bare more skin in the closed rooms. The *laissez-faire* attitude of the owners means as long as we kick them thirty percent of the fees for those dances, they don't care what any of the girls do in the rooms. I'd find it sleazy, but the girls who work here are highly skilled performers who choose to make thousands of dollars a night rather than peanuts in some ballet troupe or chorus line.

By the time I've flirted my way to the VIP tables, the Cobra is staring intently at all of us. Spotlights pin each one of us on the floor at the bass hits, and I swivel my hips as my free hand slides down to the secret spot on my jacket. In unison, we tear the jackets off to reveal rhinestone studded bras with straps criss-crossing our waists like shibari ropes. A lift of the fedora and pop of my hip, along with the beat, draws the fierce-looking brawler's eyes directly to me. I pout prettily and stalk towards his table with the swagger of a tiny dicked asshole that owns a monster truck.

His thin lips pull back over the famed curving fangs he had implanted. Dark, glittering eyes follow every move I make as I approach, and I pretend to whip my hair from side to side as I check for his guards. They're here somewhere, but I need them to be far away so I can beat my escape before they notice. When I get within inches, I tap his leg with my cane and spin around to shake my ass in his face. The grunt of approval makes me want to heave, but I turn, holding onto the prop with both hands. My feet click on the floor in a soft shoe step as I make 'fuck me' eyes at the dirty bastard. He leans back, his pants tented as he gestures towards his lap.

Fucking gross.

I don't care about his weapons trade or what happens when people get the shit he moves. I have no clue why I have to take him out. The reason they have sentenced him to death isn't part of my contract, and I'm nothing if not a dispassionate observer of the darkest parts of human desires. Twelve years at *l'Academie* ensured I care very little about anything that isn't directly related to my ability to complete my jobs.

Sighing, I dance closer and drop onto his rather unimpressive erection and wiggle. There's plenty of cloth between us to prevent him from doing anything I'd make a scene over, so I focus on the task at hand. I slip the cane behind his head, resting the wood against his neck as I tug him forward. The move reads as playfully bringing his face to my breasts, but at the last second, I click the release built into the custom weapon. One end slides open to reveal the razor sharp garotte and before he can say a word, I yank it through.

Faint gurgling is the only noise besides the end of the song, and I carefully slide the sides of the cane together. Climbing off the nasty fucker, I put my hands on his cheeks so I can pretend to flirt with him while I arrange the head so it looks as if he's leaning back in the booth. It needs to look realistic to allow me to return to the stage with the others. When I have it settled, I back away from the booth, blowing fake kisses as I walk backwards through the crowd. I almost collide with a dark-haired guy with his collar pulled high as I head for the stage, and I roll my eyes. Whatever celeb that is trying to keep their face away from the paps is doing a shitty job of it.

The entire troupe takes a few bows and shuffles off of stage left to the wings. I exhale a sigh of relief when the next group enters on the opposite side. I haven't heard shouting yet, so I don't think the Cobra's men realize he's down. Now I take this emetic pill, have a vomiting episode, and I'll get sent home.

That's when Arabella Montaigne, the burlesque dancer, will cease to exist, and Remy Arsine Benoit will re-emerge.

I smile to myself as I chew on the tablet that will have me retching my guts out in a few moments. This is a more complex extermination than I usually prefer, and I can't leave my normal calling card behind. The Cobra's head had to remain in the booth rather than get delivered to his home in a basket.

Such a shame, that. I quite enjoy the reactions my little gifts engender when they're discovered.

Walking into the dressing room, I carefully strip my costume off, putting all the pieces in my bag. Every item in the locker room that belongs to gets placed in the duffel carefully as I wait for the effects to hit me. It won't do to leave loose ends, even if my prints have never touched a single surface in this place. My gut roils and I turn, facing one of the other dancers as the vomit finally comes. Gracelia screams like she's being skinned when I hurl on her and it's everything I can do *not* to smirk through the chunks.

"C'est la merde!" she shouts, running for the showers as if she's on fire.

It takes less than a minute for the owner to send me home for the night. I walk out the back door of the building with everything just as the sirens scream.

Perfect timing, as always.

I jump into the first cab I can hail, directing him to the *Hôtel de Crillon*. Their suites are the ritziest in Paris, and it's my go-to hideout when I'm here. I used to only stay in the Bernstein Suite, but some rich fuckwad purchased it six months ago. If I could track them down and beat the hell out of them, I would, but I booked my schedule until late 2025. Assassins with my skill set and accuracy are getting harder to find. They forced the old guard into retirement because they refuse to adapt to the digital age. Too many cameras, crime labs, and hackers running about to do everything Cold War style.

The future of murder for hire is millennial, people. We're old enough to be stable, but young enough to be agile with new technology. Plus, most of them are broke AF from crooked ass student loans.

It's not an issue I have, but I've been in the business since I hit double digits. You don't survive *l'Academie des Invisibles* if you haven't killed someone before the end of primary school. It's unheard of.

I was eight the first time I used the weapon that would become my signature.

Shivering, I tap on the window of the cab and bitch the driver out. He's taking a longer route than necessary to raise my fare, and I'll have his guts for garters if he doesn't knock it the fuck off. A string of curses in French erupt from him when I voice the accusation, and I slam my palm on the window with enough force to crack the plexiglass barrier. He almost drives into another car, but when he regains control, he makes the requested adjustments to our route.

We arrived at the front entrance after a few more arguments and a traffic jam around the *Champs*. I throw the euros at him in disgust, memorizing the medallion number for later. He's not worth my time, but I have quite a few contacts who might be interested in blackmailing a cabbie in town. Getaway cars are cliche in the crime world now. Most ne'er-do-wells like myself find greater comfort in anonymous taxis or ride-share accounts hacked through the deep web accessed on burner phones. If your ride doesn't know you're a villain, there's no one to flip if law enforcement comes looking.

I never look the same for any job—ever.

I will not use Arabella Montaigne as a cover in the future, and once I move to the location of my next job, I'll ensure that she meets with a terrible fate. It's a lot more work to slowly kill off my alters once I've used them, but it's also why I've never even come close to being caught. The dancer with long wavy red hair, freckles, and big green eyes will never grace the streets of Paris again after I hop a plane. She will, however, get a minor story in the paper and an obituary when I decide how she tragically dies.

The Guillotine will rise from her ashes and be reborn.

Sneak Peek: Children of the Moon

PROLOGUE

Twenty-one years ago…

A powerful wave of apprehension hits me as we approach Claridon's house. Pausing at the edge of the forest, I wait until we can see what awaits us. The silence is deafening as we take in the wreckage of what was once the home of our dear friends.

They splintered the heavy cabin door in pieces littered around their yard like an explosion sent the shards flying. When the wind shifts, the foul stench of death and rot slams into us, making my wife gag. Lights are flickering ominously in the shattered windows and another scent—burnt food—catches the breeze as we approach.

"Cast protection before we reach the porch," I murmur.

"Ego invoco deus ab mihi. Protego mihi ab hostili et malum.[1]"

I nod solemnly, repeating her words to invoke our Goddess' watchful eyes on me as well. The scene in front of the house does not inspire confidence about what we will find inside.

The air is thick as we step onto the porch and another smell wafts towards us—blood. Its metallic tang invades our senses almost to the point of tasting copper on my tongue. Climbing over the debris, I look at the once cozy living area. Shredded cushions, torn drapes, stuffing, and other destroyed furnishings lie scattered around the room. When I bend to examine the destruction, I find coarse animal hairs embedded in the remnants. I pick some up to sense the aura of the creature it came from, but all I feel is death.

The bloody hoof prints puzzle me—I do not recognize them as belonging to any creature I'm familiar with. Whatever came to this house was not a normal shifter, nor was it a common magic user. The level of malice and lack of emotion concerns me. Its aura is like that of a necromancer or one of their creations.

I follow a set of heavy prints to the hallway leading to the dining area and kitchen. Swallowing hard, I prepare myself for the carnage I know will appear. The rotten food and decomposition scents are so bad I have to raise my shirt to cover my nose before I vomit.

It is certain our friends are dead; no one can lose the amount of blood that coats the surfaces and walls while staying alive.

"What made those claw marks? I've never seen such deep furrows," my wife whispers.

I shake my head, holding a finger to my lips to keep her quiet. I've never seen that type of mark, either, but we don't know if there's anyone still here. We must stay silent while we explore. The food on the stovetop is burned and has flies on it—that's the rotting smell. Wood is barely burning in the oven, just a few embers remaining, but it tells me our friends were caught unaware.

It means the malevolent being that attacked the wolves did it within the past few hours.

My heart stops when I remember their baby girl. Feray had to be here when it happened; it's the New Moon and both of her parents stay home during the start of the new lunar cycle.

"Freya, forgive me. I almost forgot the baby," I hiss at my wife.

Her eyes widen and her hand flies to her mouth. I see the tears forming as she thinks about what the condition of this place means for a defenseless infant. Together, we leave the kitchen, intent on heading back through the outer room to the stairs.

Just beyond the landing, we stumble over the body of Claridon. His corpse is mutilated, but I recognize those battered hands anywhere. He clearly put up a hell of a fight to keep the intruder from making it past him. Despite that, it ripped his chest open and his intestines are hanging out. Blood spatter decorates the once lovingly decorated walls, painting them vermillion and signaling his desperation to protect his family.

Swallowing again as I look at Imogen, I tilt my head at the trail of bloody hoof prints that lead to the nursery. We were here when they found out they were expecting, when they assembled the room, and even after Feray was born. Now the beauty of that memory has been sullied by the scene before us.

We have to be strong...

Once we're both ready, we follow the prints to the door of the baby wolf's room. The sight that greets us is horrific: it splayed Lyra out as if nailed to a cross and impaled her head on a post of the baby's crib. Blood is dripping down the whitewashed wood, making its way to the pink carpet. Dead eyes stare sightlessly at us as we hold our breath and enter. The injuries to our friend are a testament to how hard she fought to protect her child, though in the end, she also failed.

I don't want to see what this monster did to the baby we considered a sister to our child. Forcing myself to approach, I stare at the empty crib in astonishment. There's no sign of Feray, nor that it harmed her in this room. I whip my head around to look at my wife in shock.

Was this a kidnapping? Why would they kill everyone so brutally instead of simply sneaking in to snatch the baby?

My eyes dart around the room until I reach the closet. I stalk over, throwing the door wide. There's a pile of dirty linens and blankets in the bottom, which is unlike Lyra. She always kept everything tidy, so much so that we all teased her about it. Tossing the clothes over my shoulder, I dig down until I reach the floor. I call for light and my magic brightens the dark space enough for me to see a tiny seam at the baseboard.

Claridon was always paranoid, and I never understood why. We both lived simple lives in a small town of magic users and shifters, well outside the dangers of the big city. He was a master craftsman and Lyra ran a bakery; there was nothing to worry about. Humans were far away from our little town and the stench of corruption from the gangs and Councils doesn't exist in Silver Falls.

But I recognize a bolt hole when I see one, so I search frantically until I find the lever that will spring the door open. It takes several tries to successfully open the door—Claridon was top-notch at his trade—but when it swings out, I gasp.

There, wrapped in her father's shirt and Lyra's clothing, is Feray. She has the warding amulet Imogen made for her on her chest, and I realize that even while scared for their lives, Lyra and Claridon ensured the beast wouldn't find their child. Between the magic of our amulet and their scent swaddling her, the baby is hungry and tired, but safe.

I lift the tiny infant out of the hole gently, my eyes filling with tears. Her baby scent makes my heart hurt for my fallen friends and I clutch her to me tightly. It's our responsibility to take care of her now; I know that. Imogen nods when I look at her with a sad expression, then walks over to the dresser, opening a drawer. When she hands me the baby sling, I know she feels the same.

Once I secure Feray to my body, we make our way back to the stairs and head out of the house. It will need to be burned to keep that creature or anyone else from following the scent trail to our home. We don't want anyone to know Feray is alive; she will be safe with us as long as we continue to have her wear the amulet that suppresses her wolf.

Raising her with our daughter, in a new town, is the only way to keep her alive.

I didn't wake up this morning knowing I'd have to abandon my entire life and our home, but I know as surely as the sun will rise tomorrow what we must do to protect this baby. Looking down at her curiously, I ponder the situation again. A magical beast used as an assassin seems like overkill if their target was the infant. Slaughtering her family was also unnecessary—that thing could have slipped into her room and killed her before anyone knew it was there.

Lifting the magic on her amulet for a moment, I wait until Feray opens her eyes. That's when I realize why my friends put it on her. My wife walks up beside me and runs a finger over her cheek. Her red hair looks very much like mine and as long as we keep the magic refreshed for the spell, she will look as though she is our natural daughter.

"We must pack up and move immediately," Imogen says as we walk out. "The capital city is vast, and no one knows us there. That will allow us to raise her as our own—a sister to Fiadh."

"Yes," I murmur. "I will send a message to the local council to inform them we are moving. The death of our friends and their daughter are too much for us to bear here. You simply need to keep her secret in our home until we leave."

She nods. "What about the monster who did this? Who would send it to kill a baby, and why?"

"Someone who scared Claridon enough to make a secret bolt hole in the nursery and forced Lyra to ask us for that amulet. I don't know what they were up to, but obviously, it was much bigger than our tiny town."

Imogen frowns. "We made three amulets, love. Why weren't Lyra and Claridon wearing theirs?"

"I don't know, Gen. Whatever the reason was, they took theirs off and someone powerful hunted down their daughter. Nothing is what it seems here, but we must protect Feray. We will keep her wolf suppressed for as long as possible—up to her Ascension if we can. She'll grow up and if she's destined for something bigger, she'll be able to assume that mantle when she's ready."

Taking this baby on and keeping her secret violates our coven laws; we both know it. Hiding her means we will always be on the run—we need completely new identities when we flee to the capital. It's a lifetime commitment, but the look on my wife's face tells me she's certain this is the right thing to do.

I know without a doubt that being was pure evil, and it came with one purpose: *assassination.*

Tomorrow, we begin our lives on the lam with two babies—there is no other option .

Get it now: **https://books2read.com/ newmoonrisingCOM1**

Sneak Peek: Veiled Flame

LOSER

Kat

The little blue icon on my app has been glaring at me all day, but I'm too damn nervous to open it. Everyone at Woodlawn High has been buzzing all day with their notifications and the squeals of joy and moans of despair were too much for me to take. My anxiety is through the roof—this is the moment I've been waiting for since middle school, but I can't seem to force myself to bite the billet and check.

Maybe it's because I don't have the support system most of my classmates have?

That's probably true, given I've always been a loner and I don't fit into any specific 'caste' here. It's hard to make friends when you get shuffled from foster home to foster home over the years. I've rarely stayed anywhere long enough to make a friend, much less a group of them.

I'm not delinquent or anything—the families I've been placed with just return me like a pair of pants that doesn't fit after a year or so. The caseworkers click their tongues sympathetically and hunt down a new placement, but I've never been given a reason *why* people don't want me around. One lady said I must be born under a bad sign and hell if I knew what that meant other than I'm not good enough to keep around.

It would be different, almost understandable, if I misbehaved or got bad grades. But I don't—I'm always in the top five percent of my class and I do everything I'm asked. I don't even lord my smarts over the other kids or adults. Being presentable and unassuming was something I adapted long ago to improve my probability of staying in a home long term.

Unfortunately, it never worked and though I should be a shoo-in for scholarships and acceptances galore, I can't bring myself to be rejected yet again.

So I wait for the last bell of the day, slinging my bag over my shoulder and trudging home to the latest in my temporary housing. I can't even contemplate looking at the possible heartache waiting for me in the college application system WHS insisted we use. The fear is too great and despite knowing I'll be on my own for good at the end of this year, I'm unable to risk the pain.

I hate being this way.

My court mandated therapist says it's some sort of attachment disorder that's common in foster kids, but I think that's bullshit. The problem isn't *me* not forming attachments; it's asshole adults not forming one to me. Being left at a safe haven in a fucking basket as a baby wasn't because *I* did anything wrong—again, fucking adults couldn't handle their commitments.

As usual, I arrive home to an empty house. There are two other kids who live here—Bryce and Blake—but they're at football practice. Of course, the Jamesons *love* them; they get to strut around at games because their strays are the stars of the team. I'm not mistreated, but I'm definitely an afterthought. Both of my 'parents' are still at work, so I drop my bag on the couch and head for the kitchen to get a snack.

Don't get me wrong. I *could* have been placed in far worse homes than any of the seven I've been in since elementary school. None of the ex-fosters starved, beat, molested, or abused me. They were all decent folks with jobs and houses that weren't hellholes, but they never liked me.

I have no idea why. I tried to be everything they wanted.

But when the end of each school year came, I was handed in like a textbook and off I went to some group home until the next contestant stepped up. It baffled everyone, not just me, but that's what happened every single time.

Sighing, I pull some fruit out of the fridge and grab a soda. I have homework to do and if I want to have time to work on my stories, I'll need to get it done before the house is full of people at dinner time. Bryce and Blake will have gotten messages about their applications, too, and I'd bet my pinkie toe those idiots got into some big sports school. Brett and Allison will be oozing happiness for them and I don't know if I'll be able to keep food down if I have to admit my failure when they ask.

Being eighteen sucks ass.

After I grab my books and tablet, I head down to the den. I have to give my current parents credit; they set up a very nice workspace for us to study in the converted basement. By the time they took me in, the Jamesons created a cozy room down here where the three of us could relax and do our work for school without being interrupted. It might have been more for the boys than me, but I appreciated it all the same. Desks, a couch, big chairs, and bookshelves fill the space, making it almost seem like our mini-library. They even put a small fridge for drinks and snacks in case we had to be up late to cram.

It's my favorite place in the entire house and I spend most of my time here.

I sink into the huge armchair, putting my drink and snack on the side table. It only takes a few minutes to arrange myself in the soft cushions and I pause to tug my headphones out of my pocket. Music always soothes my jagged edges and I need it to stay focused on the bullshit AP Calculus I need to keep my average up in. My course load is heavy, but I applied to tough colleges. I wouldn't have a chance to get in, especially on a scholarship, if I wasn't taking equally challenging classes in comparison to all the prep school kids.

As always, the sounds of Vivaldi carry me away as I scrawl equations on my screen and before long, thoughts of the blue notification completely fade away.

"Kat!"

The shouts barely register as I continue working on the problem set, gnawing on my lower lip in concentration.

"Jesus fuck, where is she? I could eat a hippo!"

"Kat!"

Thumping followed by what could pass for a stampede of elephants jerks me out of my math filled trance when Bryce and Blake come down the stairs. They smell as bad as the aforementioned pachyderm's cage, so they must have rushed home right after practice. The blond twins glare at me as if I'm the offending element despite being sweaty and covered in dirt and grass stains.

This doesn't bode well.

Usually, they're tired and hungry after practices so I'm used to cranky ass boys, but tonight, there's a light to their faces. That had to mean they've gotten their letters and dinner will be a gush fest in honor of their perfection. I'm going to need all of my strength to fake smile and nod as Brett and Allison fawn over them.

I don't begrudge them their success—not really. They work hard and play even harder on the field. It's not their fault they're the American dream teens and I'm the nerdy basement troll no one wants. But it's awfully hard living in the shadow of their bright light, especially when I'm no less intelligent or talented.

"I'm finishing the AP Calc, guys. What do you want?"

They roll their eyes at me before Blake scoffs. "It's not due until Monday. You're so hyper."

Duh. I take anxiety meds, douchebag; of course I'm 'hyper.'

"I can only be who I am, Blake." That earns me a snort from Bryce and I know it's because he thinks that's the problem. "Is dinner ready?"

"Almost. Get upstairs and set the table so we can shower—Brett's orders." Blake grins smugly.

The two of them seem to always arrange it so chores get passed to me for some half-assed reason and this is no exception. Sighing, I put my stuff aside, fully intending to hide down here after the dinner mess is cleaned up. Likely by me, but like I said, I could definitely live in worse foster homes so I let it go. Doing some chores isn't worth risking the group home for the last few months of my high school career.

They take off running up the stairs and I wait for them to disappear before I follow suit. My phone is tucked in my pocket and I feel like it's a stone of shame I have to bear. I know once the adults make over the twins' success, they will remember me, and I'll be forced to find out what disappointment lies in wait for me. The dread weighs on me, but I head into the sunny kitchen and pick up the pre-prepared pile of plates, silverware, and napkins on the counter.

Allison looks up from the stove and gives me a half-smile, nodding as I take the dishes into the dining room. Like I said, no one is mean or horrid, they just seem…obligated. After a while, it makes it hard to waste time trying to be bright and sunny. Being reserved makes it a hell of a lot easier not to feel rebuffed when they don't pay attention to you regardless.

"Make sure you include champagne glasses for your dad and I!" she calls from the other room.

The twins definitely got acceptance somewhere big. Brett must have gotten the bubbly on the way home.

Once I set the table, I return to help Allison bring out the roast and sides. I'm a little amazed at her efficiency when it comes to getting the housework done while working full time, but I suppose it's something people with real parents get taught as they grow up. My home life has been so fractured that I haven't learned how to cook more than very basic shit from YouTube videos. That may be a problem after graduation, but I've never felt comfortable enough to ask Allison if she'd teach me. I'm sure she would try, but it doesn't feel right.

"How was school, Kat?"

I look over my shoulder, seeing Brett in the entry to the dining room. He's already changed from work and smiling, but I see the distraction in his eyes. He's waiting for the boys to come down. "It was fine. I've got a Calc test at the end of the week. I'll be studying a lot to get ready."

"Good, good. No matter what happens with applications, keeping your grades up will ensure no one pulls any offers," he says.

Those words aren't for me. They are for the two wet haired boys who just appeared behind him.

"Kat's too much of a geek to ever let her grades slip, Dad," Blake says as he pushes past his brother and drops into his usual chair at the table. "Grab me a Powerade since you're in the kitchen, mouse!"

Both Brett and Bryce stare at me and I turn around, heading to the fridge despite the fact that I was *not* closer than the other twin. Out of habit, I take two of the drinks and a soda for myself. I've been here long enough to know Bryce will send me back to get him one as well. It would feel like typical sibling stuff, but for some reason, I just *know* they do it to fuck with me. I have no idea why I feel that way, but trusting my gut has been the one thing that helped me get through all the upheaval in my life over the years. It's a good gauge for knowing when I'll get booted or if people are being earnest in their reactions.

The therapist says that's some sort of trauma induced early trigger warning shit, by the way.

After I hand out the drinks, I sit down on my side of the table and we wait for Allison to come out. Brett is at his seat at the far end of the table and the twins are punching each other as they look at something on their phones. I know where this is all going but I drop my gaze to the table, swallowing the coppery taste of fear as it courses through my body.

I'm going to be exposed and there's nothing I can do to stop it.

Read it now!

NOTES

HOT FOR TEACHER

1. Hurry, my love

SNEAK PEEK: CHILDREN OF THE MOON

1. I call on the gods. I protect myself from enemies and evil

About Cassandra Featherstone

Cassandra Featherstone has channeled her lifelong passion for writing into a flourishing career, a journey that started when she first grasped a pencil as a gifted child with ADHD.

Her debut novel, born during the solitude of COVID lockdown in March 2020, draws on a tapestry of personal encounters and insights that resonate deeply with her readers.

An international bestseller, Cassandra has topped Amazon charts in categories such as LGBT Anthologies, LGBTQ+ Mystery, and Bisexual Romance, among others. Her works navigate the complexities of bullying, PTSD, body dysmorphia, mental health struggles, personal reinvention, and the empowerment of claiming one's own space. Importantly, Cassandra offers a thoughtful and respectful portrayal of LGBTQIA+ relationships, subtly reflecting her own connection with the community through her narratives.

Her literary repertoire spans sci-fi fantasy, urban fantasy, paranormal, and comedic genres in academy whychoose settings, with a strong commitment to portraying consensual, safe, and accurately depicted BDSM and kink lifestyles. Her books are an invitation to explore transformative stories that are both inclusive and engaging.

Often affectionately called 'The Muppet' for her wacky theater kid personality, she resides in the Midwest with her tech-savvy husband, their creatively inclined college student, a literary-minded dog, and four scheming cats.

READ MORE AT CASSANDRA'S WEBSITE OR HER FACEBOOK PAGE. SIGN UP FOR EXCLUSIVE CONTENT AND UPDATES HERE.

FIND HER ON ANY OF THE SOCIAL MEDIA BELOW AS SHE *LOVES* TO CHAT AND *NEVER* SLEEPS!

THE MISFIT PROTECTION PROGRAM SERIES

Road to the Hollow

Return to the Hollow

Home to the Hollow

Rejected in the Hollow

Revealed in the Hollow

Healing in the Hollow

Revenge in the Hollow

AUDIO OF THE MISFIT PROTECTION PROGRAM SERIES

Road to the Hollow

APEX ACADEMY CAPERS

Come Out and Prey

Let Us Prey

In Prey We Trust

Oh Holy Spite (3.5 novella)

Eat. Prey. Love.

Prey It By Ear

AUDIO OF THE APEX ACADEMY CAPERS SERIES

Come Out & Prey

Let Us Prey

In Prey We Trust

TRANSLATIONS OF THE APEX ACADEMY CAPERS SERIES

Come Out & Prey (German)

Let Us Prey (German)

In Prey Trust (German)

DISCORDIA UNIVERSITY

Veiled Flame (Book One)

Quiet Burn (Book Two)

SECRETS OF STATE U

Blood on the Ice (Book One)

Suspicions on the Stage (Book Two)

VILLAINS & VIXENS

Bloodthirsty (Book One)

Ruthless (Book Two)

Wicked (Book Three)

AUDIO OF THE VILLAINS & VIXENS SERIES

Bloodthirsty

Ruthless

TRIANGLES & TRIBULATIONS

Hoist the Flag (PQ)

Yo-Ho Holes (Book One)

**CHILDREN OF THE MOON-
WITH SERENITY RAYNE**

New Moon Rising (Book One)

Waxing Crescent (Book Two)

Waxing Gibbous (Book Three)

Full Moon (Book Four)

Waning Gibbous (Book Five)

FAETAL ATTRACTION

Hell on Wheels (Book One)

Book Two Title TBA

RISE OF THE RESISTANCE

Ream Exclusive Prequels

Hooked on a Feline (Book One)

Peacock Me Like A Hurricane

Book 3 TBA Title

REAM SERIALS

Secrets of State U

Discordia University

Denizens of the Dark

Faetal Attraction

Agents of the Ouroboros

Rise of the Resistance

F.E.A.R. Academy

ANTHOLOGIES

Unwritten

Shifters Unleashed

Jingle My Balls

Love is in the Air

Silent Night

Snowed In

All Hallows Eve